I0690711

QUATERMAIN

THE NEW ADVENTURES

VOLUME TWO

AIRSHIP 27 PRODUCTIONS

Quatermain:The New Adventures Volume Two

"The Rose of Fire © 2016 Thomas Kent Miller
"Call of the Hunter" © 2016 Erik Franklin
"Stones of Blood" © 2016 Alan J. Porter

Published by Airship 27 Productions
www.airship27.com
www.airship27hangar.com

Interior illustrations © 2016 Clayton Hinkle
Cover illustration © 2016 Graham Hill

Editor: Ron Fortier
Associate Editor: Jaime Ramos
Marketing and Promotions Manager: Michael Vance
Production and design by Rob Davis.

ISBN-10: 1-946183-05-9
ISBN-13: 978-1-946183-05-7

Printed in the United States of America

10 9 8 7 6 5 4 3 2 1

QUATERMAIN

THE NEW ADVENTURES
VOLUME TWO

TABLE OF CONTENTS

THE ROSE OF FIRE
(FROM A MEMOIR
BY ALLAN QUATERMAIN)
BY THOMAS KENT MILLER

It was Christmas morning 1871. I was preparing to leave the Black Kloof, the dreadful, dark and haunted gorge that was the home of Zikali, "The Opener of Roads," the formidable and clever black dwarf who was the wizard Zulu kings most held in awe. Zikali had me stay for several days and nights at the Black Kloof telling him every last detail of my recent adventures to Heu-Heu land—where he had sent me to procure a certain medicine for him. As I say, I was preparing the oxen and wagons to leave the area when two of his immense guards came to me and explained very politely in their Zulu language that Zikali wished to see me one additional time before we rode off.

Now, when Hans, my faithful Hottentot servant, heard this, he clamped his hands to his head and moaned, "Baas! Oh Baas, leave now while we have the chance. No Baas! The Opener of Roads must have another grocery errand for you down another long road and I am sick to death of his errands."

Hans was a little Hottentot fellow who had been my companion through most of my adventures, even when I was a lad, as he was aide-de-camp for my father. Hans was strong, quick, and agile, also clever—extremely so—and quite astute when the need called for it. Otherwise, he remained quite content to drink when he could, and when he couldn't, he tended to get himself into mischief in the most ingenious ways. In any case, his eyes were always bloodshot from the drink, which was, if he had any choice in the matter, gin, which he called "square-face" after the shape of the bottle it came in. Nevertheless, he was devoted to me, as he was to my father before me. Sad to say, he is gone from this world now and I miss him, but that is another story and neither here nor there, and has no pertinence to my tale.

So it was that I looked at the two enormous men who stood waiting patiently and said to Hans, "If you think either or both of these fellows will take 'no' for an answer, then you may be my guest in the execution of your plan."

"No, Baas, for I think now that you have a point and because I think 'execution' is just the right word to describe our poor futures if we deny these huge fellows."

The end of it was that I was soon once again seated before the shriveled old dwarf, who said, "Macumazahn"—which means "Watcher by Night" and is what the natives call me— "thank you for returning to speak to this Old Cheat, as I know you call me at every opportunity. There is another matter of which I wish to speak.

"The reason I called you back is this: last night as I slept, my spirit flew much farther than it does most times—halfway to the stars it seemed—and when I looked down upon the face of the world, I saw not the world of forests and mountains and deserts that are the coin of the world, but instead a giant bowl, its edges aflame. Then fiery stones fell from the sky with horrible roaring sounds and poisonous smoke and crashed into the bowl."

I sat listening to this nonsense, wanting only to be on my way, for the truth is I become impatient with Zikali and his ilk very quickly. "So what does this have to do with me?" I asked. "Do you have another errand for me?"

"Why, Macumazahn, I am talking about how your life, as pale and feeble as it is, as humble as it is, will soon have an encounter with the gods, or rather, a god. That much I know from the dream. But let's look further into the matter."

Here he grabbed some ashes from the circle of dying embers that surrounded the small fire that burned forever it seemed before his crouching figure, poured them on the dirt floor and patted them flat. I should say here that my acquaintance with Zikali began when I was quite young, hardly a boy, but even then he looked much the same as he did during this encounter, a shriveled dwarf with eyes of fire and an enormous head from which granite white hair fell in lavish braids. I have often thought that this particular posture of his, which I dare say is, except once when I was about nineteen, the only one that I can recall seeing, made him look much like an evil, aberrant toad.

He clapped his hands, and a servant appeared, one of those who had requested our return, with Zikali's catskin medicine bag and handed it to the wizard, who rummaged inside and pulled out his yellowed knuckle bones, those that he kept near him at all times and used for divining, or at least supposedly so, for I don't take much stock in such tricks that are the stock in trade of Africa's wizards. Then he shook the bones in his cupped hands for a bit and threw them down into the ashes.

Here he did something that I certainly didn't expect, and can say in truth I never witnessed before or since. He actually flinched as though startled. This was especially unusual because Zikali's whole existence was one of control. In many ways, he was like the puppeteer who controlled the marionette strings of his minions over all Zululand and beyond. I pretended I hadn't noticed and he continued to peer at the bones in the ashes.

"Ah!" he said, "more than a mere encounter. Much more. You will become an honored familiar to a great goddess. No, not a great goddess. *The* Great Goddess," he said, cocking his head and glancing at the bones from a somewhat different angle. Here he began to chant under his breath in a hypnotic wavering drone and rocked back and forth on his haunches. I sat impatiently for several minutes waiting for him to say what he had to say. I must have dozed, for the next thing I remember is seeing that he had a figurine cupped in his hands. The figurine, only about three inches in height, was one of those fertility goddesses that one sees so often these days in drawings of artifacts that have been dug up from archaeological sites all over the world. This, as those, possessed heavy drooping breasts, wide hips and a pregnant, prominent belly. Zikali dug a small indentation in the ashes and there placed the figure carefully before him. He then waved his hands in wide large movements, fanning the fire and bringing some of the smoke up from the fire to himself where it circled his head then drifted down to the figurine and began to encircle it, a horizontal ring of smoke that formed a kind of halo above that bit of carved black stone. All this while he had been chanting, and after some time, it was almost as though he had gone to sleep himself, with only the occasional audible mutter communicating that he may be alert still.

His murmuring eventually stopped, and he stirred himself and coughed. Then he reached into his medicine bag again and withdrew a handful of roots that he began to deliberately place into the fire, one by one, and each flared with a different colored flame and smoke. In a few moments, a rainbow of flames emanated from the little fire and the small hut was thick with the complicated, changing patterns created by the intermingling columns of many-hued smoke.

Before long I thought I was seeing an image in the congealing smoke. It was really quite a complicated illusion, and I must admit that for a short time I almost believed the image was real. What I thought I was seeing was this: I was standing alone on an enormous plain, when suddenly a burning stone fell from the sky with a shriek, hitting the ground and setting fire to a nearby thorn bush. Then, lightning flared all around the flickering flames of the bush and a voice like thunder spoke my name, "Allan, O Allan!"

And I responded in my dream with, "My Lord, why have you brought me hither?" At this, I began untying my boots and awkwardly slipping them off my feet, for it seemed the right thing to do, though I felt rather foolish.

"O Allan, she who is mother to all, she who is mother to all the world needs your aid. Go to her and I charge you with her care while you are with her. I also task you with discharging the great responsibility that she will require of you."

"What responsibility, Lord?"

And the response was an enigmatic one. The voice from the fiery bush said, "You are but a cog in the wheel of life and in the fullness of time you will exercise my will, though mayhap you will not know it."

At which point the fiery bush began to smoke terribly, and then the smoke was the smoke in the hut. It was choking me and I had no choice but to jump up and run out into the air.

When I returned some minutes later the smoke had cleared. By what manner it was done so fast I don't know. I was feeling somewhat better then but still confused and shaken. I returned to my sitting position in the dirt before Zikali. I noticed that though the fire still flickered—for it never went out entirely—it was now mostly glowing embers and the bones, small idol and medicine bag had been cleared away. Zikali himself was motionless but making a peculiar sound. In time I decided he was laughing, "Ho, ho, ho, ho!" When he quieted down, he said, "O, White Man, who is so brave as is his whole race, I can see into your mind. You are saying, 'He is nothing but an old repulsive cheat and magician. I saw nothing of consequence except that which was suggested to me while I was somehow drugged and made to dream.' But you are also wondering now how can 'the thing that should never have been born' know of such things?

"Verily, Macumazahn, I had little to do with any of this. I have heard that your people have something called a magic lantern that projects pretty pictures that you all gather round and make surprised sounds at. Consider then that I have only been a magic lantern through which one greater than I caused you to see that which you were intended to see."

By then, I was vastly confused and said as much. But it really came down to one simple question: "Zikali, why did you want to see me and ask your messengers to bring me back here before you? Always you want me to help you for some selfish end. What do you want of me?"

The old wizard finally stopped laughing and peered at me with his infinitely black eyes. "O, Macumazahn," he began, "you always think so poorly of me! I have nothing to gain, nothing at all. The information I convey will merely be of use to you, that is all. It appears the goddess has honored you and requires you to carry a grand message outside the bowl, for that is where you will meet her, that bowl that I saw in my dream last night."

"What is this bowl?" I said, then added skeptically: "What is the nature of this message?"

"Ah, Macumazahn, as always you doubt your friend, the Old Cheat. But perhaps this time you are more justified than usual, for I can tell you no more. The fiery stones, the bowl, the queen of the gods, the message . . . these are all that I am allowed to be privy to and no more, no more details at all, for a vast black shield blocks my arts. It is as though something or someone wished to whet both our appetites, and, once having done so, withdrew.

"Now be gone with you. Though we are friends of decades, at the moment you tire me, and I want to consider what power it is that can turn the great 'Opener of Roads' into a mere tool."

Shortly thereafter, Hans and I were soon back at the wagons, where my men had made the final preparations. The oxen and the wagons were ready to go, for which I was thankful because I wanted to be away from the Black Kloof as fast as my feet and the feet of our oxen could take me.

I spent the better part of several days trying to understand what had happened. The most amazing thing of all is that, for the first time, I saw the great Zikali seem contrite and not in control. Never in my presence before or after that affair did he seem so unsure of the ground on which he stood. I alternated between shaking my head in wonderment at that and trying to make sense of the vision I saw, or thought I saw. It was almost as though the Hebrew God "I am that I am" took a moment off his busy schedule to ask a favor of me!

Dash it all! My head hurts when I pondered all this, so after a while I pushed all else out of my mind except the glorious image of a hot bath in the simple tub in my small home in Durban, the small home I had not seen in nearly a year, for that was the length of Zikali's little grocery trip!

As we approached Durban on the very day of Epiphany, 6 January 1872, the town had a merry appearance, still in the throes of Christmas celebration. I remember how all this Christmas atmosphere and a generally melancholy mood (somehow imposed on me by that damnable wizard!) put me in mind of the history of the area. Europeans had first troubled themselves to notice the southeastern coast of Africa on a Christmas morning in the fifteenth century and the area had been called Natal ever since as a consequence.

I remember too how I mused that Lieutenant Francis George Farewell would hardly have recognized the trading community he founded in May 1824, which he called Port Natal, but which name was changed a few years later to Durban, after the then new governor of the Cape. Not only had it become a prosperous and bustling town (rather than the half dozen or so poor structures that Farewell's people had thrown up) but, at the moment in question it was so festooned with decorations of the season that it appeared more a carnival than a serious community.

"Baas," Hans said while rubbing his dirty, sparsely stubbled chin, "I hope the Big Baas in the sky can forgive you your sins for which his Son was pinned to a tree, since you don't look like a man who is in the mood to celebrate anything at all, least of all His Son's birthday."

I'm never likely to forget the reason for the frown that had so changed my face that it prompted Hans's remark: there in front of my house stood three very serious, business-like men, which was precisely what I did not want to see at that time. I was tired after a very long trek and only wanted to settle into my little house, but somehow I knew that particular small reward would be denied me.

"Look yonder, Hans, and tell me what there is to celebrate."

"Oh, Baas, those three have faces like the Predikant, your reverend father, when he would find me drunk behind the shed—stern and unsmiling—but your father never had a face pale like plaster as these do. All my poor life I have known white men, both high and low, but these men are more white than any of the others, and therefore all the more ugly for it." Then he grinned, "But they also look rich, which can only be good news, as I have heard you mutter to yourself that our purse is poor and even more so since we have used up so much on this journey and gotten no reward for our grocery errand except a pat on the back from The Opener of Roads."

"Hans, I don't care if they offer me a golden platter heaped with diamonds, I intend to rest and intend to do exactly so and nothing more."

By this time, we had arrived at the proximity of my front porch, and the men in question approached. One separated himself from the others and held out his hand to me. "Mr. Quatermain I presume?"

"You are correct," I said as we shook hands.

"Mr. Quatermain, my name is Richard Holmes. I am with the British Museum. These are my associates Thomas Huxley and Sergeant Cuff."

Mr. Holmes looked as though he represented a museum. He was average height—meaning that he was somewhat taller than myself—middle aged and scholarly. His cheeks held thick tufts of graying hair and his hairline receded, but he was otherwise clean shaven.

Huxley's face was nearly covered with thick white whiskers, though his chin and cheeks were clean shaven. I said, "Mr. Huxley, your name is familiar, but I fear that I can't immediately place it." But then I remembered, "Oh! I have it now. Aren't you the man who has stood at Mr. Darwin's side through thick and thin?"

Huxley seemed pleased with this perception and my phrasing of it. "Indeed I am," said he. "Though I must admit some surprise that in a spot so remote you would have heard of my humble efforts on behalf of my friend and his conclusions."

To which I responded, "Though I may be a backwoodsman, I've read of your championing Mr. Darwin, sir, and admire your courage for standing up for what you believe. Though my reading of books is limited mostly to the Old Testament and *The Ingoldsby Legends*, I have read abstracts of Mr. Darwin's book and have seen enough in Africa to admit that his notions have given me much food for thought, at the least. I have read about you more than once in the various publications that make their way here to Durban. Though I haven't been near a newspaper in almost a year, I recall that 'survival of the fittest' is the phrase that the gentlemen of the press seemed to enjoy trumpeting about."

"Yes, indeed, sir. 'Natural selection' is still quite the topic these days."

My response was to smile politely.

As for the last member of the party, Sergeant Cuff (and now that I think about it, I don't believe I ever learned the man's Christian name—how odd!), he was of advanced age and average height. But my initial reaction was for this man's health as well, for he was hardly more than skin and bones. Beyond this, it was clear that he had not shaved for several days, his hair was gray and cut extremely short, and his complexion was severely wrinkled and dry.

Just as these thoughts crossed my mind, Hans, who had been able to stealthily come up behind me, whispered in my ear: "Oh, Baas, this one you must be careful with. He is like a dead man who still walks and talks. Do you think he might be one of the spooks who belong to The Opener of Roads?"

"Hush!" I said as unobtrusively as I could. Then to Cuff, "Mr. Holmes introduced you as Sergeant, sir. Are you retired from her majesty's service?"

"Oh, no, Quatermain. I'm a policeman."

"A policeman! What on earth?" I shook my head in confusion. "Gentlemen, gentlemen! I'm afraid I am most perplexed."

"Mr. Quatermain," Cuff rejoined, "it falls upon Mr. Holmes to explain the details at this early juncture."

Holmes opened his mouth and I'm sure would have told me all about it, about Cuff and all the rest of their business, but I would have none of it. Just then, suddenly, I was filled with a sense of defeat and perhaps a little foreboding, and it was all I could do to smile politely. I was not pleased at this uninvited, unwanted attention, but I could see that these were determined men with a mission, though at that moment I had no idea what that mission might be.

"Gentlemen! Not yet!" I said, surrendering to the feeling of fate about to overwhelm me. "I'm sure you have far more to tell me than my poor head can hold for the moment. Please allow me! As you see me this moment, I have not crossed the threshold of my house for nearly a year, and there it is, just a few feet away, beckoning me, and I'm afraid its allure is far more than I can handle."

This statement shocked them all into apoplexies of apologies, and they quickly stood back and let me through.

"You see," I began, actually enjoying the tiny bit of power I was able to assert just then, "I am anxious to take off my boots and sit in my chair. And the last thing I want to hear at the moment is your purpose. I beg you, therefore, to indulge me while I settle back into the domestic life."

🌿 🌿 🌿

After we all shared a simple dinner of buttered rice and mutton, washed down with local beer, I finally consented to hear out my unwanted guests. Hans, who had disappeared at the start, as he was wont to do when "customers" first made their appeals to me, reemerged and silently settled down onto his haunches unnoticed in a corner.

Richard Holmes began: "You know of course, just four years ago, Britain sent a large force to Abyssinia for the purpose of rescuing hostages from Emperor Theodore."

"Yes, I was upcountry during those events, but I learned of the Ethiopian campaign belatedly."

"Some 280 ships unloaded 32,000 men and 20,000 mules, and materiel enough to keep them all going. Quite an astonishing expedition. Field-Marshal Lord Napier marched his army into the highlands for some three months. In the end, Theodore took his own life (or seemed to, which is one of the reasons we're here). A certain amount of bounty was acquired for the purpose of paying the men. I can proudly say that I accompanied this expeditionary force and was there when the emperor's treasury was cataloged."

"Plundered is more like it," broke in Huxley. "I hear the soldiers went through the place like mad beasts."

"True enough, I'm afraid," responded Holmes, frowning with the memory. "In the end, however, I was able to retrieve some 900 manuscripts, a few ancient scrolls, and other historical documents to return to the museum for preservation. It has been my great and fortunate honor during the interim to examine and determine just what we found."

He had paused, for effect, I think, but since he failed to continue, I felt obliged to speak. "And this has to do with me in what way?"

"After the demise of Theodore," Holmes continued, "the three chief contenders to the throne warred amongst themselves, and still are for that matter. Her Majesty's government, for various reasons, supports one by the name of Kasa Mercha, who has been extending his influence for well over a decade. In fact, in about two weeks, it is intended by our government that he ascend to the throne. I believe he has chosen the name Yohannes IV. Naturally, this has been a long time in development.

"But in recent months rumors have reached Mercha, and thus to the top levels of the British government, to the effect that Theodore is not dead. That the dead man we came upon on the steps of his fortress Magdalawas that of a fanatical look-alike. There is talk amongst Ethiopians that Theodore still lives and rules from some secret location. The talk is that the King of Kings has risen from the dead and rules.

"Mercha, as you can imagine, is a bit nervous about these rumors. His own attempts to send agents to determine the truth have failed. Her Majesty thus feels a responsibility to make the effort to put the lie to the rumors or find Theodore if he lives. We..." he took in the others with a sweep of his arm, "...are her tools in this regard." At that, Holmes ceased to talk and there was silence.

Finally, I said, "This is all well and good, gentleman, but, I repeat, what does it have to do with me? And what does this purely political matter have to do with a noted biological naturalist like Mr. Huxley here? Or a policeman such as Sergeant Cuff? Or, for that matter, a museum curator such as yourself?"

All eyes turned to Richard Holmes. He seemed to blush for a moment. He cleared his throat and continued.

"You see, Mr. Quatermain, Napier's expedition had some corollary effects. Several, as a matter of fact. First things first, though. Sergeant Cuff is here in the official capacity of determining whether Theodore is alive or dead. He was chosen because his methods of deduction have proven over and again to be of great service to the Crown. The official determination of Theodore's continued existence or not is in his hands."

Here I looked at Cuff, but he merely rubbed the growth of gray grizzly beard on his chin. As I had nothing to say to the man at that moment, I was about to give my attention back to Holmes, when Cuff addressed me.

"I see that you have climbing roses around your porch, Quatermain."

"Why, yes. I'm afraid I don't have much chance to enjoy them, though."

"Ah. Of course. Perhaps if you were around more, then they would be better cared for. I couldn't help but notice that they're only one step from the wild state."

I was stunned. I had no idea how to take this comment. Was it innocent? Was it meant critically? If so, how dare he, who hardly knew me? Such thoughts filled my brain as I stared astonished and wide-eyed at the man.

It was Huxley who jumped to the man's rescue. "Quatermain, please understand that beyond police work, Sergeant Cuff's primary passion in life is the cultivation of roses. That is all we heard about on the voyage here."

"I'm sorry if I offended you, Quatermain," said Cuff. "It's just that roses poorly tended rub me the wrong way. A year is a long time to be away, though, to be sure. And, yes, it is my affidavit that may very well put an end to this Theodore affair."

Not quite knowing what to make of all this, I took a long quiet, and what I hoped was an unobtrusive, breath and then slipped on my bartering face, the blank expression I always wore when trading with the various peoples one encounters in Africa. Unfazed by the interruption, Holmes was continuing. "Huxley's role is one of an entirely different character."

Huxley took up the tale: "You can imagine what it must have been like, 32,000 men and tens of thousands of animals crossing the desert and thence into the highlands. Though I was not there, I can see in my mind the

"…roses poorly tended rub me the wrong way."

cloud of dust. Richard was there, however, and he has described the scene. No matter the details. You see, once the army had accomplished its goals and marched back through the village of Zula to Annesley Bay, the harbor from which the expedition had been mounted, one soldier, Corporal Saint James by name, knowing it would take several days to dismantle the camp, decided to do a bit of sightseeing. You understand, his activities at that time were strictly contrary to orders, but he rationalized that he would never be in Ethiopia again and that he had a small boy back home in India for whom he wanted to find a proper souvenir. His route took him into some barren, terrible areas, as he describes them. At one point he found something of particular interest. Not being an ignorant man, he knew he had found something of interest to more than just his young son."

Huxley slowly reached into his inside coat pocket and removed a leather pouch. He opened it, extracted some wadding, which he unfolded, and produced a piece of bone, which he then held out to me. Taking note of the wadding and extreme care with which it had been packaged, I took hold of it very gingerly and held it up into the light from a beam that poured through the window into the room from the setting sun. I turned the bone every which way, showed it to Hans, and so on. But in fact, it wasn't bone at all but rock in the shape of a bone, so I knew it to be some sort of fossil.

Huxley continued, "He spotted a dozen or so pieces just such as you have there just lying on the desert floor, exposed to the elements. He picked them all up, protected them, and, of course, intended to get them aboard ship without anyone noticing."

I examined the piece closer, saying, "It looks to be the forearm bone from a monkey of some sort." I looked at Hans, who was nodding his head vigorously. "Fossilized," I added, "which implies great age. However, aside from that, I am not clear as to its significance."

"Ah, you are quite right, Quatermain," said Huxley. "It does in fact originate from a primate of some sort. You see, this is but one of the several pieces that Saint James found. It is a convoluted story, but Saint James's escapade did not go unnoticed and his souvenirs were commandeered. Fortunately, they made their way into my hands. I shudder when I imagine what could have happened to them if they had been the responsibility of less learned men. Suspecting an unusual provenance, I brought them to the attention of Darwin. He and I have spent days, weeks, with the bones, measuring, weighing, comparing, conjecturing, mulling over the whole set. The upshot is that we are convinced that these bones belong to a primitive ancestor of Man—perhaps as old as a million years. The very sort of creature Darwin hypothesizes about in *The Descent of Man*, which in fact was being printed in February just as these fragments came to our attention.

"However, our conjectures are meaningless with so little to go on, so it quickly became imperative that I needed to go to Ethiopia and more closely investigate the region Corporal Saint James stumbled upon. Through official channels, it was determined that both the need of the British government to put to bed the Theodore matter and the interests of Mr. Darwin and myself intersected and that it would be mutually beneficial if we all teamed together. Feeling grateful that there was a chance to hastily join an expedition of an official nature that was in itself being hastily prepared, I, as Mr. Darwin's representative, became part of the group you see before you today. In fact, as I had pressing responsibilities, it was necessary that I feign illness from overwork." Here he grinned. "I was so successful that my doctor prescribed therapeutic travel. Only Darwin and a few others in the government know where I truly am. To the rest of the world, I'm on holiday in France and Germany."

During this entire conference, I was sitting in my rocker, one of the items I missed the most while traveling. I rocked. And I rocked. I must tell you, there was a profound silence on the porch. I rocked because I was thinking.

Eventually, I looked again at the group's spokesman and said, "Mr. Holmes, I must admit that these various tales I'm hearing are interesting. Though, as I said, the notions of Mr. Huxley here and Mr. Darwin have given me pause, actually, I tend to lean toward the Old Testament in such matters, and besides, it seems to me that a monkey bone is merely a monkey bone. And that is the end of it. As I said, this is all very interesting, but it doesn't explain your presence, Mr. Holmes."

The face of the museum curator suddenly glowed; his eyes grew wide and he exclaimed, "Mr. Quatermain, I am present for no less reason than a miracle . . . ."

"My dear Mr. Holmes!" I exclaimed, for I was not used to being associated with such terminology.

"Mr. Quatermain, are you familiar with the Great Library of Alexandria?"

I'm afraid that my education, being rough and administered in the wilds of what is now the Cradock district of the Cape Colony, lacked such subtleties and the particular institution to which Holmes referred meant little to me. I said as much.

"Indeed, the Great Library of Alexandria was planned by the first

Ptolemy and developed in the third century B.C. by Ptolemy II. Its goal was no less than the accumulation of all knowledge, and it seemed to have succeeded in that regard. Within its walls were some 700,000 papyrus scrolls containing the wisdom of the Macedonians, Romans, Egyptians, Jews, Indians, Persians, and Phoenicians, all their religion, science, and history. Over six centuries, this library evolved into the intellectual core and splendor of civilization, the crowning achievement of human life on earth. But, at the end of the fourth century A.D., the Christian Emperor Theodosius ordered it all burned."

"My word! What on earth for?"

"Well, Christianity was so sufficiently new that Theodosius was fearful of anything pagan, which is how he thought of the library and its contents. It was not one of the prouder moments of the Christian era, to be sure." Here he paused. "Yet, as I studied in the British Museum the hundreds of volumes from Theodore's treasury, I found several references, delicious hints, if you will, that inferred that a portion of the library, or at least many of its important scrolls, were secretly packed up, removed to Abyssinia, and hidden from the book burners. Preserved, in other words. And there is every reason to believe that remnant of the library has not been touched since, that it is waiting to be rediscovered—perhaps to help humankind enter a new renaissance."

Holmes then pulled a bit of paper from an inside coat pocket. "Quatermain, let me give you one small example of the nature of the sorts of things this library may hold for us. What I have here is a translation from a fragment of a scroll I found in Theodore's treasury. It, in turn, is a copy of a scroll far older that was part of the Alexandrian Library. Now, please indulge me and read this."

Reluctantly, for I knew that by doing so I was enmeshing myself further than I desired into this venture, I reached for the paper. Yet, before I was able to touch it, Holmes drew his hand back, saying, "Quatermain, have you not heard of the Synoptic Problem?"

"The what problem?"

"In the Bible, man! Mark, Matthew, and Luke are called the Synoptic Gospels because they have such similar elements. Of Mark's 661 verses, more than 600 of Matthew's and 350 of Luke's are the same. But Matthew and Luke have 200 other verses that are the same but that do not appear in Mark."

"I had no idea," I said.

"For years, scholars have hypothesized that Matthew and Luke were independently compiled, or drawn, from Mark and from another and unknown source document. This would be an entirely new gospel."

"Yes . . . I can see that," I said noncommittally.

"What you are about to read could well be a mere fragment from that new gospel. The author purports to be one Gaspar, which is the name tradition has attributed to one of the three Wise Men. Many scholars believe that if the Magi existed at all, they were probably Zoroastrian priests from somewhere in Asia Minor. It is also claimed in tradition that Gaspar was the youngest of the Wise Men and that he was Ethiopian."

He handed me the scrap of paper, his eyes wide with expectation, and I began to read:

"Thus Gaspar says:

"These are the words of Gaspar the Ethiopian.

"I am dismayed. A significant portion of my life has been given to the study of one man, and more and more frequently I hear reports concerning him that are blatantly false or twisted far beyond the simple truths.

"Why is this? Can there be so many whose self-interest outweighs the simple truth?

"In all things, Jesus the Nazarene said, 'Treat others as you would have them treat you. Do good and give as you can without expecting a thing in return. Your reward will be great, and God will call you his children. Show mercy even as your Father shows mercy. Do not judge, for how can you judge? What right do you have to judge when you have no understanding why a person is the way that person is? Remember, the standard you use will be the standard used toward you.'"

And thus the short document ended, and when I had finished reading, I looked at the men grouped in my house. I wasn't sure what they expected me to say or do. I wanted to say something like, "Mr. Holmes, surely you have better things to do with your time than to dabble in romance writing of this inferior sort" but I thought better of it. Instead, I looked at them all and said, "I don't understand."

Holmes looked exasperated. I must chuckle to myself when I think back on it. He took the scrap back belligerently, neatly folded it, and returned it to his pocket. Then he continued as though I had said nothing. "This is only a fragment. If the full Gaspar document had been in circulation about 50 A.D.—which is when we believe it was written—then it would certainly have become part of the Alexandrian Library. Alternatively, if Gaspar was Ethiopian, then it's not entirely unlikely that a copy of his writings would have found its way into the library of an Ethiopian 'king of kings.' In either case, the full document, if we considered it and nothing else at all, would be priceless beyond discussion. And if it turns out to be the lost source document of which I was speaking, decades of arguing would be put to rest." Holmes let that sink in for a moment, then said, "But that could all be moot because we are not looking for one document but a library, or at least a significant portion of one."

As preposterous as all this sounded, I was beginning to realize that these important people hadn't come all the way from England to test my patience. "I repeat *again*," said I, "what does all this have to do with me?"

"We want you to help us find the surviving remnants of the great Library of Alexandria," said Holmes.

"To help locate King Theodore II, if he still exists," broke in Sergeant Cuff.

"And to help locate the region where I can find more primitive bones," said Huxley.

I took a deep breath, calmed down. When next I spoke it was some minutes later. "Gentlemen, I assume your passage from London to Durban was done at the expense of the British government. That is all to the good. Because what you are proposing is lunacy—pure lunacy on a grand scale for a myriad of reasons. I would have thought that men of your backgrounds would have realized the total futility of these sundry ventures, not to mention the cumulative lot, and would have given it up no sooner had the thought entered your collective minds.

"It would be one thing if you had maps or directions—though heaven knows I have seen enough suspect maps in my day!"

Holmes then muttered something, a characteristic that did not seem to become the man, though I had only just met him.

"I beg your pardon," I asked.

"Quatermain," he began again, but with less conviction, "we did bring some statements that might be of navigational assistance." He drew some more papers out of his coat pocket. He shuffled through them a moment, settled on one, and continued, "Corporal Saint James described his journey as well as he could. Let me read an extract from his account:

"Our thousands had been steering down from the highlands into

the base camp. I was near the end of that long column, a fact that allowed me to move around somewhat more than others without being observed. At an opportune time, when the front of the column arrived in the vicinity of the bay, I took off at dusk heading at first due south into the desert, then following the easiest path, which turned me a bit to the east. I didn't know what I was looking for, only that my boy would like a fine souvenir. The funny thing is that I didn't feel at all worried at being found out. Instead I felt more like a kid at play. Anyway, seeing that you want to know my route, after some time the moon came up and I could see my surroundings pretty clearly. I'd say it was about ten miles from the start that a range of mountains kind of popped up on my left. Even though I could see, on account of the moon, I couldn't see much. I just knew they were there . . . how far away I couldn't be certain. So far my path presented little more than broken rock and sand. Then I saw something that chilled my soul. In the distance, southwest of my position, the sky was glowing with redness, I couldn't help but aim toward the spot and after several miles I could see what looked like a boiling cauldron at the top of a large hill. 'I'll be daft,' I thought, 'a volcano!'"

Here Holmes looked up at me. "And he goes on like this describing what he saw and how he navigated between two other volcanoes. He was asked some pointedly specific questions having to do with the kinds of rocks he noticed, type and degree of vegetation, etc. Unfortunately, he wasn't able to provide more than a middling amount of specific information, not being a naturalist of any sort. But in broad outlines, his expedition has been documented up to the point he found the fossil bones, which is the point at which he finally determined he should return. Now it is fairly certain that the first volcano he encountered was Mt. Erta Ale, the location of which, obviously, is well known and mapped. The point is that his journey can be extrapolated and his probable positions placed on a map. So you see, in effect, we do have a map of sorts leading to the general vicinity of his wonderful find."

I opened my mouth to express my incredulity, since the "vicinity" Huxley so blithely spoke of was no doubt equivalent to hundreds of square miles, but I was cut short. "But there's more, Quatermain." Here he shuffled more of his papers. "Those rumors about Theodore still being alive include some geographical detail, namely that his presumed base camp is probably near a ridge that is approachable from the east on a path that leads between two volcanoes. The entrance point of this path is about three days northwest by horse from the tip of the peninsula that is the African side of the Strait of Bab el Mandeb. Once again, extrapolating from the available information, we have reason to believe that the other two volcanoes are the Dama 'Ali and the Kurub Koma, two of a chain of mountains and volcanoes that dot that country. The camp itself is on the western side of the volcanoes. And here it gets a little tricky. No one can say if the camp is approachable from the west."

Abruptly, Sergeant Cuff broke in. "It is pure extrapolation actually. If the camp is approachable from the west, then it would be in a spot just about due south of the fossil find, perhaps fifty or seventy-five miles. Our proposal then is to use Saint James's information to locate the fossil beds, and then we turn south and try to approach Theodore's camp from the west, and if we can, determine if Theodore is still with us or not. If that proves impossible, then we merely circle toward the south and east to find the path between the volcanoes."

To say I was dumbfounded would be an understatement. Tomfoolery, tommy rot, suicide, the whole venture was. And I said as much. "Sir, I have heard nothing but a lot of very vague terms in the last few minutes, words like *might provide, middling information, broad outlines, fairly certain—* you see, I have been listening!—*extrapolated, in effect, general vicinity, rumors, reason to believe*, and now you just uttered the most foolhardy of them all. One does not *merely* circle around a pair of volcanic mountains in singularly unknown territory."

I looked helplessly at these unwanted guests of mine. I looked at each face in turn, at once trying, I suppose, to communicate with my eyes the hopelessness of this plan, and at the same time gain some sense of their degree of purpose. Indeed, all I saw was their passion and determination. I looked at the papers still in Holmes's hands that told of completely unrelated aspects of terrain in a part of the world of which I knew precisely nothing and uttered my exact sentiments.

"Gentlemen," I said testily, "I don't see how these fool scribblings will help one bit. Furthermore, what on earth do these sets of directions have to do with your great library or a new gospel?"

Holmes was the one who spoke. "Quatermain, this base camp we have been speaking of . . . Theodore's hideout . . .we think it is one and the same place where the remnants of Alexandria's library were sequestered. At least, that is the working theory of some who are positioned in the government just to make such informed conjectures. The reasoning goes thus: if thousands of scrolls could exist there safely for almost fifteen hundred years, why not one man for four years?"

✿ ✿ ✿

I was already so numb from this veritable landslide of nonsense that this new pebble hardly affected me at all.

Here Holmes looked pointedly at Sergeant Cuff. "It is Cuff's job to officially put the lie to this whole untidy affair, or, if true, give Theodore certain communications and promises. The problem is that so little is known about Abyssinia in Europe. We have the limited knowledge derived from the Napier expedition, of course, but they pursued a course into the highlands and stuck to it, while ours will lie in the other direction into the desert. Ideally, we need the services of someone with perfect knowledge of the country's geology, climate, peoples, and natural history."

"I hope you don't think I'm such a person."

"No, of course not," Holmes said. "However, we do think you are the next best thing. You, Quatermain, as very few others, are intimately acquainted with Africa, its moods, its pulse, and its people and cultures. We need you to help us in our endeavor to navigate this aspect of its exotic and strange nature."

I was quiet for a time, then I said, "I'm flattered your opinion of me is so high. Yet the truth is the truth. I know nothing of Ethiopia. As I have said, gentlemen, it's out of the question. Admittedly, I would not ordinarily refuse a commission, but I'm tired and want nothing more than to spend some time quietly in my home."

During this discussion, Hans had maneuvered himself closer to me so that now he was just below my ear.

"Whoa, Baas!" he whispered in Zulu, "We were only a little while ago talking about the Big Baas in the sky, and I see that he certainly knows more than you about your own pocketbook for he is sending you even now that big gold plate full of pretty rocks of which you were talking so recently."

And the truth of it was that Hans was correct. Our financial situation was sad indeed. The long trek into Heu-Heu land may have provided Zikali with his great medicine, which Hans was pleased to call "groceries"—by the way, this medicine consisted of leaves from a grand old tree called the Tree of Illusions, which Zikali required for his black arts—but all I profited was memories, most of which I would have just as soon done without, for there was much fighting involved and death and much sorrow . . . but that is a whole 'nother tale.

Anyway, Hans's talk had a sobering effect on me, and I found myself saying, "You have come to me to be your guide, despite my never having been to that region and having no familiarity with it or its people at all."

"Mr. Quatermain, the British Museum, indeed, the British government—Her Majesty herself, I might add," said Holmes, "as well as others—have every reason to believe that if anyone in Africa can help us, it is you, sir! They have the greatest faith in you!"

"I am indeed flattered," I said. "But what if I hadn't just arrived back to Durban, not to return for a year or more, as I am wont to do in my business—as I have just done?"

"But that isn't the case—is it?—we are happy to say," Holmes responded. "But now that you have a notion of what we want to do, shall we discuss terms? For your services, to begin in due course after you have had an opportunity to rest for a time, the British authorities will pay you—" whereupon he mentioned a sum so prodigiously ample with terms so fair that I would have been a fool to have turned it down.

Hans, who had been watching and listening the whole time, took this opportunity to whisper to me, "Whoa! Baas, such a pretty number I have never heard. Yes, our trek has been long and my feet need to rest, but perhaps our feet only need a very little rest after all."

Frankly, I was beginning to think along those very lines myself, and the end of it was that I agreed to attempt what seemed at the time to be the most ridiculous proposal I had ever heard in my entire life.

※ ※ ※

Within twelve days I was able to settle my affairs and was readying my house once again for an extended absence and preparing to board the *H.M.S. Deborah*, the British Navy vessel that had brought my clients. With Hans, I was returning from town with an armload of supplies, my home being on the outskirts of Durban, when I became aware that someone was sitting on my porch bench. A giant of a Zulu had made himself comfortable.

The Zulu jumped up when he saw me. He was naked, of course (imagine a black David), except for an animal skin about his middle and various ceremonial accouterments that hung from his neck, ears, and ankles. He held up his *assegai*, or short stabbing spear, in royal salute, greeting me by my native name.

"Macumazana, I am Bayushtiak. The Great One has sent me to protect you."

By "Great One," I knew he was referring to Zikali, but I had no idea what he was talking about otherwise.

"Bayushtiak, thank you for your diligence," I responded in the Zulu tongue, "but please return to your master and tell him 'no thank you' as I am in no need for a bodyguard."

"Oh, that is not possible, Macumazahn, for he told me that if you were to start your expedition without me as part of your party, then I would die in a dishonorable fashion and that my spirit would live forever trapped in a turtle shell without hope of escape. So you see, Macumazahn, that, unless you wish me thus, which, as you well know, would be far worse than even wandering forever in the featureless underworld, you must allow me to take care of you as a wet nurse would her mistress's baby."

Now, clearly I was offended by this analogy, but beyond that I was confused. "Bayushtiak, did your master say why I would need a bodyguard?"

"He showed me some signs and whispered secrets into my ear, but there is nothing that he gave me leave to share—not even with you."

Now, I was in an untenable position. On one hand, I had no need for protection. It was my job, in fact, to protect the others in my charge. But if I refused the man, I knew full well that the hideous black dwarf would cause the man grief somehow, and I didn't want to be responsible for that. What matter if we had an extra member in our party, and the man looked capable enough, strong, self-confident—no doubt a good man to have with you when trouble arose.

"Well, Bayushtiak, it appears that I don't have much of a say in the matter as I well understand how Zikali keeps his word. Welcome, then. But I would appreciate a word of warning when you see this mysterious danger approaching."

"Oh, Macumazahn, do not fear on that account. The Great One heightened my sight and gave me wondrous charms and medicines that will allow me to see forward when the time comes."

"Well, then," I said, feeling manipulated, "it's all settled."

🌿 🌿 🌿

The next morning, Holmes, Huxley, Cuff, Hans, Bayushtiak, and myself boarded the *Deborah*. The ship weighed anchor, and off we headed north up the east coast of Africa.

"The Great One has sent me to protect you."

I had a time of it explaining to the others about our new compatriot, for he was not the sort of companion that anyone of them was used to, but, in the end, they all accepted this unexpected turn of events, since they, just as myself, had no real control of the situation. Thus, we understand the power of Zikali.

The master of the ship was one Captain Enfield, and he took full and instant umbrage at having Bayushtiak come aboard. It offended his sensibilities to have a "savage" on the ship. Bayushtiak, for his part, took no notice of the man, occupying his time, once we had set sail, observing the world from the standpoint of the bow of the ship.

"Macumazahn," he would say to me, "little did I know that the world was so wet and big. I see that it goes on seemingly forever, and no matter how fast or far this vessel moves, even as day turns to night and night becomes day, over and again, there is still more water ahead, with no end in sight."

"Yes, Bayushtiak, such is the way of the world, or rather the planet, for they say the earth is a round ball. Naturally then, you can travel around it forever, and they also say that it is mainly covered with water, so you could travel thus forever surrounded by water." I noticed that whereas an urbanized man would soon become bored with the monotony of the endless sea, Bayushtiak's demeanor was never less than sheer wonder. Many a time I would see him there rooted at the ship's bow.

We sailed up the coast—a journey of some three thousand miles and nearly two weeks time—then eventually around the Horn into the Gulf of Aden, through the narrow Strait of Bab el Mandeb comprising Yemen on the east and Somaliland on the west, thus into the Red Sea.

Within a few more days, we turned hard south into Annesley Bay and finally came within sight of the two wonderful piers tipped with lighthouses that the English army engineers had built four years previously in preparation for receiving Napier's armada. These piers—marvels of engineering both—extended 900 and 700 yards into the sea from the desert shore. Beyond them, a few hundred yards further up on the shore, was the strange and anomalous sight of several derelict and rusted locomotives, which had been left behind by the army as it hurriedly left. Beyond these, some dozen miles away due west, the Ethiopian highlands began their precipitous climb high into green mist.

As cool and refreshing a sight as the highlands struck me just then, I knew that we would be headed south into the desert.

As we approached the piers from the east, we were very surprised to see another vessel approaching from the north. Captain Enfield was not expecting this and, as was his nature, became quite flustered. As it would have proven fruitless to even discuss or guess about the nature of this "intrusion" or "crossing of paths" or however it should be phrased, we passengers simply watched and waited. It seemed certain, though, that the other was also a British naval vessel, for we could see the colors flying in the wind through the spy glass that the captain made available to us.

The *Deborah* landed at the end of the longer of the two piers. As we unloaded our supplies, Holmes described to us what he had seen there before, comparatively recently.

"Gentlemen, just imagine four years ago, at this very spot, utilizing these very piers that he had built for the purpose, Field-Marshal Napier gathered together all his men, animals, and materiel, which included fifty elephants with which to carry the heavy guns. Once the shorter pier had been constructed, a tramway was laid along it, and the fleet began to unload.

"Can you imagine, all along the shore there was a city of tents. Thousands of Indians, Egyptians, Persians, and Ethiopians hauling supplies from the ships. Over there was the native bazaar, over there the hospital, along there the storehouses, beyond those the animal compounds with over 20,000 mules alone. Right here on this very spot on this pier and yonder on the other as well were the two condensers that produced almost 200 tons of potable water each day. You can see there where they were fastened down.

"The heat was appalling, and the flies a veritable plague. Dust stirred up by all the feet, both human and animal, billowed in the air constantly. A city popped up in the desert almost overnight. The logistics of it all were inconceivably awesome, at least to one inexperienced in such matters such as myself. The army assembled, then marched and conquered. It was hardly more complicated than that, given the anachronistic, almost barbaric, nature of the enemy. On our return, it was all dismantled and loaded back onto the ships, everything, that is, except these piers and those locomotives. The whole affair was quite remarkable."

Hans, of course, took all of this in and then offered his own brand of wisdom. "Baas, even if the Baas with the shiny chin had not said so, I could tell he spoke truly from the tent pole holes, the droppings, and all the rest of the spoor. Even four years has not been enough to make all these things new again. Just think, Baas, it would be like all of Durban here one moment and gone the next!"

It was about this time that the other vessel reached the piers and secured itself. Captain Endfield, my clients, and myself, all stood by, our curiosity at a peak.

It was not long before some people disembarked and approached us. Of course, there were among them sundry mariners, but the central group comprised four men and a woman. One of the men was obviously the captain of the other vessel and he broke off from the group and approached our captain. He seemed quite happy. They greeted one another precisely and the new man introduced himself to Captain Endfield as Baker by name, Captain Joshua Baker.

"Captain Endfield," said Baker, "We were beginning to wonder if you would ever show up," which was an interesting manner to start the conversation. Thereafter, the two discussed numerous matters of consequence to the navy. In the end we learned that, for its own reasons, the British Admiralty had required Baker to catch up with the *Deborah*, and that Baker had found that using the new Suez Canal—which had connected the Mediterranean Sea with the Red Sea just two years before— made this feat simplicity itself. It made entirely moot the necessity of circumnavigating the entire continent of Africa, which is precisely what the *Deborah* had been required to do, first to pick me up at Durban, and then to continue on up the east coast of Africa. The sailing of the *Granger*, which was the name of the other vessel, had been smooth and without incident. In fact, they had been waiting for us for six days, using the time to take depth measurements off the Abyssinian coast and other assorted matters of marine research.

Now it was that Huxley stepped up to Captain Baker in a not altogether cheerful mood. "Huxley's my name, sir, and I would greatly appreciate knowing the meaning of this. Leaving Britain, as we did under the strictest orders and secrecy, nothing was mentioned of collateral matters."

At that moment, the rest of Captain Baker's group joined us. It was the older of the three other men who began to approach Huxley, but then spotted Holmes and veered right off, grinning and hand held out. He was a man in his forties. On his upper lip was a generous mustache. He was a few inches taller than myself, seemed strong and fit enough, and subsequent events would prove me correct.

Holmes and the new man shook hands, but then erupted into a paroxysm of back slapping and earthy diminutives. Then they seemed to suddenly realize that they were making an exhibition out of themselves and then Holmes turned the man around brusquely and introduced him to us: "This fine fellow is Henry Stanley. My God, what brings you here, Henry?"

Huxley brightened and said, "Mr. Henry Stanley of 'Dr. Livingston, I presume' fame? World renowned reporter for the New York *Herald!*"

The fellow held out his hand to Huxley and said, "And I gather you must be Huxley, Thomas Huxley. And these others then must be Cuff and Quatermain." He shook our hands briskly.

There was then a profound silence among our group that was broken only by the cries of the seabirds. Finally, like a dam bursting, we all began to talk at once. Realizing the futility of this, we all stopped, and it was Stanley who came to our rescue. He looked back at Huxley and said, "Yes, to answer your question, it is I who wrote those dispatches to the *Herald.* The good doctor was difficult to locate, but you know what they say about perseverance!"

Holmes was quick to say, "I can only assume that there is an excellent reason for all this, Henry."

Stanley indicated the three other people who had accompanied him off the ship. "You're right there, Richard. At least your government seems to think so. But let me introduce the rest of my party. This charming lady is Professor Maria Mitchell, and these two chaps are Gunnery Sergeants Daniel Dravot and Peachy Carnehan." I noted with interest that the professor's Christian name was pronounced "ma-RYE-a" rather than "ma-REE-a" as one would suppose.

They both saluted smartly at the sound of their names and the one called Dravot stepped forward. "Of the Queen's own royal infantry, Indian Army under Field-Marshal Lord Napier, SIR!" he added forthrightly. An immense man with a full flaming red beard, he reminded me rather of a Viking of old. He stepped back and joined his mate Carnehan, whose own distinguishing characteristics were his bushy dark eyebrows that went clear across his forehead without a break and shoulders that were as broad as Dravot's beard was red.

Stanley went on, "The Crown has loaned us these two fellows because of special knowledge that is theirs. Since the four of us are embarking on a quest instigated at the request of Professor Mitchell, I'll let her explain."

Maria Mitchell smiled at my group and spoke with a distinct accent (my American clients have had many different accents, and I wasn't able to identify hers just then). "I should be happy to, but shall we first retire out of the sun to a more comfortable situation with plenty of room to spread out."

The two captains graciously offered accommodations on their respective vessels, and finally we were led to the officer's briefing room aboard the

Granger. We were quite a group, I must say. When we were all settled—Bayushtiak choosing to stay on deck to continue his examination of the world's girth, and Hans as usual, crouching unobtrusively in a corner—there were Captains Endfield and Baker, myself, Holmes, Huxley, Cuff, Stanley, Dravot, Carnehan, and, of course, Professor Mitchell. All these men and a woman who had mysteriously come together and assembled in this simple room on the edge of the closest thing to the middle of nowhere that I could imagine, all by the will of the British government.

Except for Professor Mitchell, who stood, and Hans, we all somehow fit around an oblong table. She appeared to be in her fifties. Her countenance was expressive but entirely severe. Her hair, which was dark and beginning to gray, was pulled back into a tight knot. Her clothing matched her countenance in both tone and style, being dark and severe with only a white lace collar to add a little diversion to the whole.

"My name, as you know, is Maria Mitchell. Some of you perhaps have heard of me. Certainly my name doesn't have the cachet of Mr. Stanley's, nonetheless, in some scientific circles, my name has some meaning. For instance, Mr. Huxley and Mr. Holmes, I would be very surprised if neither of you know of me."

The two men thus addressed rose to the occasion. Huxley cleared his throat and sat rather more tall in his chair. "Certainly, Professor Mitchell," he began, "I have the pleasure of addressing the eminent professor of astronomy at Vassar College in New York State. I believe it was in 1847 that you discovered a comet, a fact that remained newsworthy for nearly a year. I was but a lad at the time, but I remember it well."

Miss Mitchell smiled and was about to open her mouth when Holmes also took up the challenge as well. "If I recall correctly, professor," he began, "your particular fields of interest are sunspots, the surfaces of Jupiter and Saturn, and meteorites."

"Indeed," she responded, seeming pleased, "correct on every point, and it is the latter interest, that of meteorites, that brings me to Africa and to this very spot conferring with you gentlemen at this very moment. I've come in search of a phenomenon unheard of thus far in the study of meteorites. This phenomenon came to light in 1868 here in Ethiopia and was witnessed by these two men," indicating Dravot and Carnehan. "Gentlemen, please do me the honor of taking up the tale from the beginning."

The two men stood and snapped to attention just as though an officer had barked an order. It was Dravot who started.

"At the beginning, all right. Well there we were, Peachy and me, happy as could be. Stationed in Bombay we were and glad of it. We were gunnery sergeants; we were, under Field-Marshal Lord Napier in the Queen's own Indian Army. Well, next thing we know we were boarding a ship and weeks later landed at the very same God-forsaken spot where we are right now, pardon my language, Ma'am. And soon, in a matter of mere days, as I live and breathe, a whole town popped up . . . . " Holmes took this opportunity to interrupt, a bit impatiently. "Dravot, my man, the details of the camp are well known to us and not important at the moment."

Dravot looked a little abashed as though the wind had been socked right out of his sails. Seeing that reinforcements were required, Carnehan stepped in. "Be that as it may, Danny here and me at some point considered all the problems and difficulties that lay in the direction of the general march, which was northwest up into those very mountains outside there, but which wouldn't seriously start moving for several days, and we decided to explore a bit in the opposite direction, to the south it was, which we found was truly horrible desert country, as you will soon see."

Dravot took it up. "And it was when we were out there in the desert more than a few days, glad to be away from the hubbub yonder in the mountains—a lot of bloody shooting and such—that the miracle happened."

"Not that it was rightly a true miracle," interrupted Carnehan, "but it came with all the accessories, a great light in the sky and loud noises from heaven, as God is my witness! But I suppose it was really that we just happened to be in the right place at the right time. It was about midnight, we were bivouacked in a dry riverbed where we were toasting the Queen, bless her heart, when it exploded out of the sky, it did, and streaked toward us, scaring the stuffings out of us."

Dravot took it up again. "It was a meteor, as you live and breathe, a real spectacular rock shooting from the sky. What with all the blazing and crashing and whistling and all, it was quite a show it was. Well, it hit off to the east of where we were, and not too far. So in the morning we went looking for it, and blimey, what we found was queer enough to get the whole ever-lovin' government to wondering, which explains just why Peachy and me are right back here."

"And just what did you find?" I asked, by now bursting with curiosity.

"Why a graveyard of meteorites, of course! Have you ever heard of the graveyard of the elephants or of the whales, well this is much the same thing, hundreds of craters each with a bit of charred rock half buried. We found the new one, all right. It was still red hot from its plunge, but otherwise it didn't seem any different than the others. They all seemed part of a family if you don't mind my conjecturing. Well, we scraped around a little and found some interesting pieces, having no notion as to the value of the things, and pocketed them."

"The wonder of it," Peachy continued, "was that when we went back the way we came and merged into the tail end of that long column the front of which was days ahead high up into those mountains, no one seems to have noticed that we'd been missing."

Dravot interrupted in a precisely timed manner. "My thinking, y' see, was that they were glad to be rid of us! After all, it wasn't as though Peachy and me didn't have a pretty thorough reputation!"

"So there we were, possessors of this most arcane knowledge," Carnehan continued. "'Danny,' I said, 'what are we to do now? You and me, we've been bloomin' witnesses to a true-blue wonder of nature. So what's next?' Well, there was nothing next. At least immediately. That was four years ago, and we gave up trying to figure out how to make a profit, so to speak, from our discovery, but tongues being what they are, word got 'round and bits of our rock got 'round, too, and lo! some months ago, this lovely lady here communicated with us. We've never asked for details, but it must have been a pretty picture, she digging through those layers and layers of government bureaucracies in order to find the likes of us. But bless it! She did, and here we are, loaned out by the Queen herself to help this here lady seek that very exact same spot of our bloomin' miracle."

"Thank you, gentlemen," Maria Mitchell said, continuing. "Naturally, one of the first things we attempted to do was to contact Mr. Holmes here to request his guidance and aid due to his previous experience in the area. It was then we discovered we had missed him by a matter of only a few weeks. With the aid of the Museum authorities, we were able to contact Mr. Stanley, who, auspiciously for us was still in England having just met with the Queen, on the one hand, and who had been part of the expeditionary force four years ago, on the other."

"As a reporter for the *Herald*, you understand," Stanley felt obliged to say.

"Given his familiarity with the area, we explained that his companionship and guidance would be of great service, to which he kindly agreed. We, nonetheless, were firm in our belief that Mr. Holmes's services would be invaluable. In due course, we were able to compute the probable course and timing of your northerly expedition from Mr. Quatermain's home and realized it was highly likely to rendezvous with you via the Suez

Canal. And, at long last, here we are, altogether, by the grace of the great God Himself."

Dravot and Carnehan told us that their "graveyard" was three or four days forced march south-south-east, which was in the same direction that Saint James had indicated he had gone, though the two adventures had been separated by some weeks, one at the beginning of the army's expedition and one at the end.

"Like it as not," Dravot volunteered, "seeing that it was just the two of us, Peachy and me made good time. We wanted to do our sightseein' and be back before we was noticed missing and in enough time that we could come up with a sensible excuse. But with the likes of this crowd, with a lady and without a gun in our back, so to speak, it's probable to take twice as long, at least. Six, maybe seven days." Dravot shrugged, looking for all the world like a man who, for the moment, had no control at all over his destiny.

Well, there was nothing for it now. Once the direction of travel was made clear, as well as the terrain and climate we would encounter, taking into account that we wouldn't have bearers, we spent the day choosing and packing our kit, which consisted of the following items: nine express rifles and six hundred rounds of ammunition; two Winchester repeating rifles (for Hans and Maria) with two hundred rounds of cartridges; ten Colt revolvers and two hundred rounds of cartridges; eleven Cochrane's water bottles, each holding four pints; ten blankets (Bayushtiak eschewing such frivolities); ninety pounds of biltong (sun-dried game flesh); a couple hundred small dry biscuits; a selection of medicines and a few small surgical instruments. Our knives, compasses, matches, pocket-filters, some tobacco, a trowel, sundry digging tools, and the clothes we stood in completed our supplies. Later, too, I discovered that Stanley had brought along his surveying equipment to which he was much attached.

In my experience, which in many African matters is substantial; this allotment of equipment was modest for the desert adventure we proposed. These were the bare necessities. Nevertheless, every ounce, I knew, would seem to double as the trek lengthened. Even still, it was a heavy load per person. Obviously we would not allow Miss Mitchell to carry a full load, as she did not seem by nature to be an outdoors woman, and so approximately half of her kit was distributed among the others. She protested vehemently, but soon gave up as we men were not about to give in.

What I had no way of telling at that time was what a *vital* woman she could be when her back was against a wall. In a few days her mettle would be tested and she would prove to be much more than she seemed.

As we were all making these final preparations, double-checking our supplies, etc., Hans stepped up to my side. "Baas, tell me again why it is here I am going to die, cooked like an ostrich in an oven," he queried in his insolent tone. "I don't understand why these old books and old bones and rocks from the sky are worth all these fine men and that lady turning themselves into hyena food. Of course I don't count myself amongst those fine men, but unless I am mistaken, I too will join them in the hyena's belly."

"You silly fool," I whispered harshly. "If worse comes to worse, I would grab the hyena's throat and eat him, and thus we would all live."

"Baas, the people hereabouts call you 'Macumazahn,' which means 'Watcher by Night,' not 'Uhlanya Ngokweqile,' which means 'Mad Beyond All Reason.' I beg you to remember that if you were to grab the hyena's throat, he would try to tear out yours and in all likelihood would succeed."

Naturally I was not about to take such language, even from Hans, so it was that I said not too kindly, "How dare you waste my time with your silly nonsense," all the while as the toe of my boot strove to encounter the seat of his filthy pants, but he was too quick and jumped liked a startled rabbit. But this was more of a long-standing and time-honored ritual between us than anything else and the next time I saw him, neither of us thought to mention the matter.

We had become quite a swollen group to be sure. At first, I thought I would have to fight with Stanley for my rights as safari leader, but he was perfectly happy for me to take the lead, which I was grateful for insofar as I wasn't in the mood for political nonsense at that time.

Thus, we made arrangements with the captain of the *Deborah* to return to this spot beginning in three weeks, wait a week, then return after another three weeks, and so on for four months. During the extended intervals, the vessel would be performing mapping and surveying duties for the British government. The *Granger*, we all agreed, had concluded the business that it had with its four passengers, and we discharged Captain Baker to continue on whatever other Queen's business he was obliged to pursue.

We decided to avoid the heat of the day and to travel by moonlight. And so it was in the late afternoon, deep in shadow since the sun had dropped behind the mountains on our right, we headed directly into the

"….we headed directly into…the Danakil Desert…"

heart of one of the loneliest, bleakest spots on the face of the earth, a vast area of barren wastes, broken lava flows, crumbling rock, and salt flats known as the Danakil Desert—a truly hellish place, arid, monstrously hot, torn by volcanoes, and prone to earthquakes.

That first night we passed over patches of uneven gravel and greenish sand rich in copper and through fields of broken and jagged black obsidian. As hard to traverse as it was, it did have the advantage of being relatively flat.

At dawn, we entered a different realm altogether, one of torturous, steep gullies that rolled away from us like endless waves to the horizon. One notable feature of these gullies was the vibrant colors they presented—deep reds, bright yellows, translucent greens, browns and blacks, and aquatic blues, all arrayed in pleasant stripes along the gully walls. I assumed this was due to the fact that, as in many deserts, it seldom rained here, but when it did or if there was a heavy rain, however short in duration, in the mountains to the north or west, the water would rush in torrents that funneled into these gullies, vanishing afterward into shallow salt lakes that, in turn, soon evaporated. But in the wake of these floods, the sides of the gullies and ravines would appear riven, as though a giant's axe had cleaved asunder the old tired and worn walls of rock, revealing shiny new, thick layers of rock of distinctly different colors and character, minerals from distant eras, from epochs unimaginable.

Yet as fearsome as these gullies seemed at the time, it turns out they were relatively shallow and nondescript compared to the region we would soon encounter—but I'm getting ahead of myself. We halted on the south side of an east-west oriented gully that was deep enough that it could almost be called a shallow canyon. There was some discussion that perhaps it would be better to make camp on the bluff above, for in the event of a flash flood, the water could roar down on us with the speed of an express locomotive, and also because, typically, gullies and canyons in this climate tended to be hot and stifling. But due to some trick of nature, that gully at that time enjoyed a steady and comfortable breeze coursing along its length, and, added to the relief afforded by the shady side, in the end gully won out over bluff and we settled into our first camp, which was plain and practical.

We supped on some of the provisions we'd brought, drank warm water sparingly, and fell into conversation. This was the first opportunity we'd had to actually get to know one another, and I was rather curious about this assorted lot that it was my fate to have fallen in with.

Huxley sat against a boulder writing in what I guessed was a journal.

Richard Holmes and Miss Mitchell chatted, she making expansive gestures. Dravot and Carnehan were prowling together around the edges of
the gully. Detective Cuff, Hans, and Bayushtiak stayed more or less off to
themselves. So it was that Stanley and I gravitated to one another, as our
backgrounds had points in common.

"Quatermain, I say, I've been wanting to meet you for some time," said
the famous journalist and explorer. I replied, "Well, sir, it appears that
your wish has finally come true. I, too, have heard much of you."

Thus we exchanged anecdotes dealing with the travails of our chosen
careers, neither feeling particularly comfortable, I suppose. Eventually,
knowing that rest was more important than talk, I went about the posting
of a guard, Dravot I believe, and the rest of us settled in, preparing as
best as we could for the heat of the coming day. In my own fashion, I was
asleep before you know it, it being my nature to be able to sleep under any
circumstance, hard or soft, wet or dry, hot or cold, imminent danger or
not.

In the late afternoon, we ate, broke camp, and set out once more. Before
two hours were up, we came to some of the most desolate and forbidding
territory I had ever encountered or could imagine. Suddenly, we could see
in the bright moonlight a vast and frightening region comprising wide
gorges and ravines and hills cut into the wasteland by wind and the action
of prehistoric rivers. It was truly astonishing to see these nearly vertical
five-hundred foot dips and rises, one following another like wrinkles in a
titanic rumpled blanket out to the horizon as far as the eye could see.

We consulted Dravot and Carnehan and they were adamant that they
had, in fact, encountered this very same landscape and had not found it
necessary to traverse it. Those four years before, they veered further south
and had succeeded in circumnavigating the gorges. Indeed, as we marched
through the night, the treacherous terrain smoothed out somewhat.

Needless to say, from the start of our journey, Huxley had his eyes
riveted to the ground at all times—both as we marched, of course, and
particularly when we stopped—searching for the bones of the human
ancestors he coveted.

At dawn we settled into the second camp of our expedition. It was as
we were preparing to sleep that detective Cuff spoke to Professor Mitchell.
"Perhaps you can explain to those of us not acquainted with meteors, falling

stars, and such, just what you are seeking and why. Please understand that this whole detour, so to speak, was not part of my charter, and I need to come to terms with it." Well, I must tell you that appeared to be just the right question, for, just as though a coin had been inserted into a player piano, the lady then gleefully launched into what amounted to a lecture.

"Well," she began, "let's define our terms at the outset. If you see a streak of light in the sky, what you are seeing is a bit of material from outer space possibly no bigger than a grain of sand entering our atmosphere at a tremendous speed, possibly around 20,000 miles per hour. Its substance encounters the particles of air in our atmosphere, and at such a high speed, the pure friction caused by the encounter burns the material, vaporizing it out of existence causing a bright streak in the sky called a 'meteor' or, less accurately, a 'shooting star.' These flaming bits of sand constitute the vast majority of the meteors that we see.

"Larger chunks of material can also be seen as meteors as they plummet through the atmosphere, but these are far fewer than their smaller brethren. Many of these are sufficiently big that only the outermost layer burns, then some part of the original material survives the superheated furnace as they enter the atmosphere and crash to the ground. Once the surviving material hits the ground, that material is called a 'meteorite.'

"Virtually all meteorites to the naked eye of laymen look no different than ordinary rocks. Nonetheless, they can be categorized into three groups—stones, irons, and stony irons, with the stones being by far the most common."

It was left to Hans to ask the most obvious question and, of course, he directed his query to me. "But, Baas, in my head I can see a picture of rocks falling out of the sky, some burning all up, some not, but where do they come from?"

Miss Mitchell was quick to reply, "My good man, meteors and meteorites can originate almost anywhere beyond the earth—the Moon, perhaps, or the other planets, comets, asteroids. Over time, these bodies tend to jostle about and shake off the stones and irons that hurl through space for millions of years. Some eventually reach earth and, well, now you know what happens."

Hans lifted his filthy hat and scratched his scalp, his perplexed countenance not having changed. I knew that later I would need to concoct an analogy that he could understand, seeing that matters of even the simplest astronomy were excluded from his world. Dear me, in fact, I could only just grasp some of the concepts that the woman was tossing around so blithely. Twenty thousand miles an hour, indeed. Just what does "outer space" mean anyway? Then it was that I asked something that tugged at my mind.

"Professor Mitchell, just why aren't we beaned by these falling rocks on a regular basis?"

Professor Mitchell smiled. "That is a wonderful question, Mr. Quatermain. Actually, it is estimated that only a few dozen meteors per year survive the journey. And the earth is so vast that the majority of these fall into the ocean or into the ice of the poles or into virgin territory of one sort or another. The chance of being struck by a meteorite is astronomically small." She smiled again, perhaps at her play on words.

"And now that we have the benefit of this explanation," I went on, "please tell me again why we are searching for this graveyard of yours, or rather that of our two imaginative soldiers yonder."

"That can be simply stated," she replied. "The examples of the rock that Mr. Dravot and Mr. Carnehan brought out of this desert were of the iron variety. The description of the region the men provided leads me to believe that most, if not all, of the meteorites they've seen are irons. So the principal question arises: Why do so many of these iron rocks from outer space come to earth in such a concentrated manner? Is it the region that somehow attracts them? Or is it their timing and trajectories that somehow cause their falls to be focused?"

I then suggested they sleep, and that I would take the first watch.

Frankly, I wished Cuff had kept his question to himself, as I didn't like the aching in my head that followed this discourse on subjects utterly foreign to me. As I have said, I am a simple man with simple needs, and the notions that were being thrown about that dawn were such that I would have been very pleased to have avoided them altogether.

※ ※ ※

Thereafter, we left the land of gullies and canyons behind and the volcano—Mt. Erta Ale, if I haven't mentioned the name already—grew steadily more prominent in the west. Nevertheless, despite the proximity of an active volcano, the terrain became less rocky and more sandy. Indeed, most of that night the going was made all the more difficult due to the fineness of the sand and the fact that our progress was intermittently blocked by vast sand dunes.

Our trek for the next day and night meandered across a sere landscape not remarkably different from the drab, blistering desert we had been traversing all along. Just as we were setting up yet another camp, Huxley approached me and asked my opinion of a certain geological feature that he had noticed on a rise a bit to our south. I peered at it through my glass and offered my opinion that it seemed to be a small cave. He then determined to explore it, and I admit my curiosity was piqued so I went along. The ground there was particularly broken, not sand at all but shattered sandstone. The rise was steep and we climbed hard as we aimed for the cave.

Then Huxley noticed something partway up the slope. He stopped and peered at it without touching it. "That's a bit of arm from a sub-man . . . a troglodyte perhaps," he said.

"I think not," I said. "It's too small. It must be a monkey of some kind."

"Whatever it is, it is nearly human, but not quite."

I looked again. "Monkey," I said with conviction.

Huxley ignored me and pointed beside my foot. "What is that?" He squatted and carefully picked up a scrap of material and announced, "Why, it's the back of a small skull."

A few feet away was part of a femur, a thigh bone. We began to see other bits of bone on the slope: a couple of vertebrae, part of a pelvis, all of which Huxley announced were sub-human. "In fact," he exclaimed, "these are all part of one individual, parts of a single primitive skeleton."

Well the end of it was that Huxley very carefully packed up the various pieces of the skeleton in cotton and small sacks brought for the purpose. As he took measurements of the spot where he had found the bones, Stanley indicated that he had with him (indeed never went anywhere without) chronometers, prismatic compasses, thermometers, a telescope, a portable sundial, sextants, barometers, and a box of mathematical instruments, the services of which he offered. Thus, with Stanley's aid, and his surveying instruments, the precise location of the bones was determined, the better to guide future naturalists should they wish to follow in our footsteps. Also, I remember now that, in the excitement, we forgot all about the cave. Well I'm glad of that because there is little doubt that Huxley would have found some treasure or another, which would have delayed us. I insisted that we find shade and rest.

The next evening, we found that the natural path we were following led to the base of an exceedingly steep but not unclimbable hill.

Carnehan suddenly got excited. "I know this place," he said. "We're very close. Danny, what do you think? Ain't we made a bulls-eye? The devil take it if we didn't."

Dravot looked about and said, "I believe you're right, Peachy, my man. I'd venture that it was at the top of this hill and yonder a bit."

Naturally, at this news Professor Mitchell became quite animated and attacked the hill, Holmes with her, only to find that more was required than just spirit and enthusiasm. Undaunted, most of my party all began to claw up the side of what was a monstrous sand drift. We Europeans had to rest several times. On the other hand, Hans and Bayushtiak were waiting for us at the top when we arrived and had been for quite some time.

The moon had just set and there was nothing at all to see, as excited as we were to see something of this particular goal after having given so much of ourselves to the quest these last days. But, nonetheless, there was something about that particular night, I remember. The sky was the deepest black with the stars shining particularly bright, sharp, and unwavering—a sight even unusual for one who has spent the better part of his career out in the open on the deserts, savannas, and veldts of southern Africa.

Hans, who was never far from me, was even prompted to whisper in my ear, "Baas, the sky is ablaze as though Shaka's battalions were cooking a wedding feast over fires covering a field stretching from one horizon to the other."

Frankly this observation was quite accurate and I responded with, "Let's hope it is the fires of a happy wedding rather than the blazes of warriors tempering and sharpening their blades in preparation for a glorious battle, which, frankly, doesn't interest me overly much at the moment."

"No, Baas! Don't mention such battles, lest you put a curse on us all." And he made the Hottentot sign that was meant to ward off evil. Unfortunately, his effort was in vain, as will soon be seen.

Not being able to proceed further, we set up camp rather precariously on the hill's summit and slept an unsound sleep.

That morning we awoke and saw that we had, in fact, climbed to the top of a rolling plateau constituting a mixture of sand and broken volcanic rock, and from our vantage point we could see miles in every direction. As would be expected, the entire face of the desert to our left was a rolling profusion of gullies and ugly ravines. Ahead of us, along the horizon, a series of massive symmetrical cones were lined up like titanic cauldrons simmering some monstrous witches brew, proving that we were still in the midst of volcano country.

I felt it was necessary to take advantage of the cool of the morning and I insisted we continue steadfastly on. Within an hour, we heard Dravot shouting, "I see it! There, beyond that rise. Do you see the black patch? That's the beginning of it."

He and Carnehan threw down their gear and loped ahead to the spot Dravot had indicated. They were quickly at the top of that rise jumping and waving their arms and shouting. Well, the end of it was that soon our entire party had joined them, and there below us was one of the most astonishing sights I had ever seen, notwithstanding several days of concentrated astounding sights.

The two soldiers had not been making up a story, as I had more than half believed. The proof was before me—a veritable blasted valley, a scorched bowl about as wide as a racetrack and as big around. And the whole of it was filled with craters, some new, some old, most overlapping older ones and older ones still, and each crater awash in shattered black stone.

"Baas!" cried Hans. "Am I dead that I have come here to the gates of that very underworld that your Predikant father so often warned me about when he caught me sampling square face?"

The poor fellow was clearly upset. But who could blame him really, for this description was certainly quite accurate, just as his description the previous night of the stars had been. I bethought me that Hans was developing a poetic, or perhaps "dramatic" would be a better word, streak that I had not experienced before.

Still, call it the gates of underworld, or a graveyard of meteorites, or the very pit of Hell itself, whatever it was, there it was before us . . . daring us to stay away.

❋ ❋ ❋

There was no rhyme or reason to how we behaved. We all dispersed at random through that amazing field of mysterious stones from the starry reaches outside and above the earth and we wandered aimlessly as though through a maze, around the bigger stones, stepping over the smaller ones, circling the craters, kneeling and stooping and behaving like tourists at Kensington Gardens.

I heard Professor Mitchell exclaim, "Why, just as I suspected, they're almost all irons and some stony-irons, but I can't see any stones—none at all!" Then a little later I heard Holmes exclaim, "My word! There are some green ones and some with shiny bubbles that shine with miniature rainbows!"

Bayushtiak approached me then and asked, "What is this place, Macumazahn? It is like a dream world. Such rocks I've never seen in my life and have never been told about by my fathers or my fathers's fathers." You see, in the course of Maria Mitchell explaining to us the scientific background that underlay her quest, I saw no reason to translate her lecture for Bayushtiak's benefit. So, of all of us, he was the only one who arrived at this place with no preconceptions at all.

I then took a few moments to condense for him what little I understood. When I was done, his face was stern and his eyes hard as ebony crystal. He swept his arm around in a wide gesture and said, "Then these are the corpses of the stars. As I think you know now, The Great One warned me of conditions for which I must be wary." Here he looked at me with wide open eyes, indicating I suppose, secret knowledge, but I was too proud to respond in kind. He ignored my stubbornness and continued. "'Beware,' The Great One said, 'of the gathering of heaven's dead.'"

My response was calculated, of course. "Bayushtiak, my new friend, I have known you only for a few days but already I know that you are strong and stalwart and would be a great ally in time of trouble, but I don't anticipate—regardless of what your master says—that I will have much to fear from a pile of blasted rocks strewn across the plain."

His response came slowly. "Macumazahn, I don't believe that is what The Great One meant." At that, he only stood tall and proud, gazing at the cosmic field and said nothing more for a time.

When we were all sated with this new experience and Professor Mitchell had collected a number of canvas sacks full of samples, we set up camp before the sun beat down too harshly. We started a fire of ancient camel dung to heat water and prepare our meals.

Henry Stanley seemed to be bursting with his desire to share his thoughts. "It occurs to me that this spot is not that far distant from Mecca, where, of course, can be found the Black Stone embedded in the north-east corner of the Kaaba. Now this stone is thought to be the only remaining relic of the shrine used by Abraham and his son Ishmael for the worship of God, and is, therefore, considered to be the very right hand of God. But in actuality, or, that is, I have heard it said authoritatively, it is a common enough metallic aerolite—a meteorite—which I suspect is true because

Dr. Wilson, of the Greenwich Observatory once showed me a specimen which externally appeared to be a black slag but the interior of which was a bright, sparkling grayish-white which he assured me was the result of combining nickel with iron. The point I'm trying to make here is that it is possible that the Black Stone is no different from any of those yonder and that it merely missed the mark, so to speak, and fell in Arabia, which is only a bit north of here."

Stanley stopped speaking, and I have to admit that this information of his gave me much food for thought, and perhaps it did the same for the others, for we were all quiet for a time.

Richard Holmes then spoke. "Along those lines, you know, it is sometimes said that the Holy Grail, rather than being the cup most people imagine, is actually a fantastic black stone, possibly a meteorite . . . at least that's the way von Eschenbach would have it." He looked around expectantly at each of us, but as no one seemed inclined to pursue this line of thinking, he let it drop, I believe a little disgruntled if I read him right.

Professor Mitchell chose that moment to offer us some of her thoughts. "My theory is that this spot is particularly magnetic, in fact possibly a titanic lodestone if you like. If that can be proven, then the research possibilities are almost endless—between the region's natural magnetic quality and the nature of the meteorites themselves!"

Holmes spoke next. "Do you mean that as debris enters the atmosphere, those stones that are chiefly iron would have a tendency to be deflected to this spot due to the presumed extraordinary magnetism here?"

"Yes, that's precisely what I mean. Mr. Quatermain, do you have your compass available?"

Within moments, we were all peering at our assorted compasses. None of them were pointing north. They all behaved strangely. Mine, in particular, moved around in circles. Stanley's merely wobbled up and down like a seesaw.

At this point Holmes and Miss Mitchell conferred, then announced that, as Miss Mitchell had indicated, this was an unprecedented phenomenon and that this area required a team of specialists to follow and take detailed readings. What was required were trained mineralogists, chemists, physicists, and the like. Stanley then lent a hand surveying the place with his instruments and nailing its precise location for any future visit.

Then Miss Mitchell opened her mouth to say something, stopped in mid-utterance, and, to my surprise, peered at each and every one of us minutely, and even looked over her shoulder! When she was apparently satisfied, she voiced her thought: "There are even those naturalists who wonder quietly if life itself may have arisen not on earth as we all suppose, but was translated to the earth via a meteoric infection, if you will."

I believe she intended to elaborate on this notion, but I'm afraid we never heard her ideas because at that moment we were attacked.

❋ ❋ ❋

We were discussing the ramifications of the meteorites and had just heard Miss Mitchell's pregnant pronouncement—when Danakil tribesmen intent on butchering us swooped into the graveyard. We were rushed on all sides. With banshee screams, they pounced on us with their spears, daggers, and one or two rifles.

I am quite certain that we would all have been killed in short order if it had not been for the instant leopard-like reaction of Bayushtiak, who, if I haven't mentioned it before, was also called "Umoya Oshisayo Womphefumulo Wengwe Emnyama Elindile," which means, in fact, "The Steaming Breath of the Crouching Black Leopard" and was a special title of nobility—hence, invincibility —amongst his people. The very instant of the Danakil attack he was suddenly everywhere at once slashing and stabbing with his assegai, eerily silent as he went about his bloody business.

His instant single-handed defense so confused the attackers that they retreated, giving me time to disperse our guns and form the group into a defensive circle behind Bayushtiak. This had hardly been completed when the Danakil, who must have realized the error of their strategy, rushed back with murderous intent. The next few minutes were a blur of anguished screams, of dodging and thrusting, punctuated by explosions of scarlet. And in the mad confusion, somehow Hans, Sergeant Cuff, and I got separated from the others and found ourselves backing deeper into the meteorite graveyard where Bayushtiak had already led many of his attackers.

At some point, I looked and saw Bayushtiak atop a huge pointed, obsidian-like meteorite chopping and slicing at what seemed a never-ending torrent of Danakil savages. Hans was to my right and Cuff was at my back, and the three of us moved to protect Bayushtiak's rear. It was fearsome, finding ourselves surrounded by savages, dodging whirling daggers and razor-like spears.

It was deadly clear that our small defending force was severely outmanned, and I had already given up hope, I must admit. I knew as

"...he was suddenly everywhere...slashing and stabbing..."

clearly as I have ever known anything that I was about to die. While one part of me mechanically continued to blast and chop at the enemy, another part was preparing to meet my Maker, listing my many transgressions over the years and hoping I could talk my way pass the Pearly Gates.

Then it was that a great wonder happened that turned the tide permanently. At one point, two warriors broke through the circle that some of our men had formed around Miss Mitchell. But she was not a woman to be intimidated or killed so easily. She had somehow grabbed a long dagger, almost a sword, from one of the warriors and at once stepped into the fray unmindful of danger and with a perfunctory hacking of the blade sent the head of one of the Danakil rolling. Ten yards along the ground it rolled and off the edge of a nearby gully, falling fifteen feet or so into the sand below.

At this, the fellow's confederates ceased fighting to a man, turned on their heels, and retreated. So startled was Cuff by this rapid turnabout that for one instant he was caught off guard—time enough for one quick-witted tribesman to thrust his jagged dagger deep into Cuff's loins. The next instant the Danakil was shot dead by a bullet from Hans's Winchester.

A good shot, but too late, for the damage had been done. I dashed to where Cuff had fallen, ripped open his shirt, and evaluated his wound. When I had determined that he was alive, Dravot and Carnehan lifted him and carried him over to our camp.

Of course, our first reaction was to feel confusion mingled with relief. We were not then, or ever to be made, certain as to why the attack turned so fast. Hans, I think, had the best thought on the subject. He said, "Baas, what I think happened is that the warriors saw a woman behave like a man and not only defend but attack and kill. After all, it is their job to impress the women. I think that the lady's attack was something they could not understand and therefore they grew afraid, perhaps of witchcraft for all I know, and left as quickly as they had arrived."

As he happened to say this in English, he was overheard by Miss Mitchell, who, though exhausted, laughed heartily.

She said, "Mr. Quatermain, your man may have a point. All I can say for certain is that I may be a woman who men are inclined to coddle and protect, but I'm not about to stand back and let myself be killed when there is still so much to learn. The stars in the heavens above and all their brethren in all the spaces in between are my domain and I have promised the almighty God himself that I will not die until I chart their courses and know their secrets to the very best of my ability." She became thoughtful for a moment, then declared, "But all that notwithstanding, there was something else. During that time when I was so surrounded, I felt infused with some special power, something radiating from within and from without . . . something I've never felt..."

I then assessed our condition. Aside from Cuff, my group had accounted for themselves well, and by the grace of God, we were largely unharmed. We bandaged our assorted wounds and then fashioned a sort of stretcher for Cuff that we would take turns carrying, then gathered our supplies and marched on despite the heat of the day with the purpose of finding some spot where we could find shelter and which we could defend in the event of a renewed attack.

But that was easier said than done in that hellish landscape. We left behind the meteorite field, and all the rest of that day dragged ourselves across the shifting, whispering sands. Slowly, the undulating crevasses and washes flattened out and we found ourselves on flat desert again, which just as abruptly ended at the vertical edge of a plateau. We saw that the cliff ran to both our left and right for as far as we could see. The descent was at least two hundred feet, and not even Hans was disposed to attempt the climb down.

Despairingly, we headed southwest along the edge of the plateau, all the time keeping an eye over our shoulders, half expecting the Danakil to strike again, and also looking ahead for a passage down. Our march was made a little easier at this point because the plateau sloped gently in our direction of travel with the result that the vertical drop to the desert floor steadily lessened.

It was toward nightfall, then, that we saw a tiny gleam of light ahead of us. It was the setting sun reflecting off a polished surface such as metal or glass.

Hans, who tended to act as our scout and was some distance ahead of us, saw it too. He ran ahead and investigated, peering over the edge of the cliff. Then all at once, he began to shout for our attention and jump around, pointing down and jabbing with a finger. When we arrived by him and looked down where he pointed, we were amazed by the most incongruous and oddest of sights. Down below, out there in the middle of the desert, built on the edge of a wind-swept ravine, there was a sort of church or monastery mounted with a lacy delicate-looking orthodox

Christian cross, the point of which rose just far enough above the cliff to catch the sun and thus attract our attention.

There were steep stairs—about ten feet wide from edge to edge—hewn into the yellow sandstone cliff face. I noticed that they were smooth and worn down in the center, as though they had been in use for centuries. Having no choice, we clambered down. The reasons were simple enough: first of all because there was no where else to go, and second, Sergeant Cuff was clearly in need of more medical attention than we could provide in the wild, and perhaps this place would be able to help. Also, we went because we were all, every one of us, full of curiosity. I suppose we made a great deal of noise as we descended. Certainly, it was a cumbersome business hauling Cuff's stretcher down.

It was only natural then that when we touched the floor of the ravine, there were waiting for us four very formal looking fellows. All were quite black, but three were older, sporting trimmed beards like white, curly wool, wearing long purple robes and matching caps that were perfectly flat on top. The younger, but nonetheless middle-aged, man was beardless but otherwise dressed the same. They all grinned from ear to ear and seemed quite happy to see us. They were standing before the gate of a tall wall that enclosed the monastery.

As our two groups stood facing one another, taking stock of one another, I could see inside through the gate, that is to say into the further side of the wall, a most wonderful little garden filled with roses of every imaginable color.

"Well, Quatermain, aren't you going to speak to them," Richard Holmes ventured in a manner that I considered brusque.

In fact, though, at that very moment I was wondering to myself which language would be best suited when the younger man spoke first. He held out his hand to me in the Western fashion. Utterly amazed, I took his hand, and he said in English, "Gentlemen, welcome to the Chapel of the Immaculate Heart. I am Tabot Haile Mariam, and these are my brother priests. We are of the Order of Sainte Mariam the Divine. We have been aware of your coming for some days and are full of questions as to what would bring you here to us in the desert, which I daresay is, and I can say this with some authority, without doubt the most terrible spot on earth. Welcome."

"You are most kind," I responded, seeing that the Englishmen and the two Americans in my party were all grinning with relief (as I myself felt, though mystified) at hearing our own language spoken.

"Ah, you are wondering how it is that I speak English well. That is simple. When I was a child, some other Englishmen much like yourselves were seeking the source of the Nile and stumbled on my village, which was on the northern shore of Lake Tana. They tarried there for two years studying our way of life and religion and, being a quick study and nimble, I became their go-between or messenger."

This exchange had taken only a moment, and I thought that his explanation seemed reasonable enough. He was about to say something more when it seemed they all noticed the wounded Cuff on the stretcher for the first time. Two of the older men suddenly became totally solicitous and began to minister to him at once without saying a word. Cuff, who was conscious, tried to say something, but one of these priests hushed him by placing a finger over his parched lips. They lifted the stretcher and gingerly carried Cuff through the gate.

It was then that a most unexpected and, thinking back on it, a most wondrous, though predictable, thing happened. The two priests had only gotten about halfway across the rose garden, when suddenly their patient managed to cry out. "Stop!" he called. "Stop, I say. I must see this place!" You can imagine how startled the priests were. In fact, they almost dropped the stretcher, I think. But Tabot quickly translated, and they set the stretcher gently enough on a sort of rock bench that happened to be there.

Cuff was struggling to lift his head and look all around. His face seemed to glow, which was odd given the circumstances, and then he started to rave: "What a rosery! ("Rosery" is the word Cuff always used for "rose garden.") A rosery fit for a god. Just the right exposure, yes, south and sou'-west. How do you achieve adequate water in this hellish place? I must commend the gardener." He craned his head up and around, and even though the struggle was apparent and you could almost feel his pain, he ignored all protestations and peered around in as much of a circle as he could. "Ah. Even here, there is clear sign of advanced civilization. See the shape of this rosery—it's a circle set in a square. That is a fine design. And the paths between the beds . . . . Oh, I see they are crushed rock . . . well, I suppose that must do in this region, but beware! Roses do not like being surrounded by rock. It is hard on them."

Thus he waxed about the infrastructure of the rosery for a time, and then fell silent. It was just as the priests were about to pick up his stretcher again that he blurted out once more. "See the colors, whites and reds and yellows. And, oh, there are the blush roses. They mix so well together, don't they?"

At that he seemed to drift off, and the priests were able to continue with their task of moving Sergeant Cuff indoors. My emotions were many, I must say. Perhaps it was not too late to save the man. But I put all that aside for the time being and turned my attention to Tabot. "Yes, Tabot, your desert does test the most hardened and intrepid. Of that there can be no doubt. In fact, we have only a few hours ago been battling for our lives, and some of us have wounds that need to be tended to, though I daresay that the one you have already taken in, Sergeant Cuff by name, is already being helped by your doctors."

"True enough," said Tabot. "We will help him as well as we can, though I cannot promise anything. Now, tell me: What on earth brings you here?"

"That is a very long and complex story, I fear," was my reply. "I don't mean to seem rude, but the telling of it should wait until we are rested. For now, let me just say that we are explorers seeking knowledge."

Tabot chuckled at this and said, "There is a saying in your world, I think, something about getting blood from a turnip. That, I think, is the amount of knowledge you can get from these sands," gesturing out across the desert. He said something to the remaining priest and they shared a good laugh. "Do come in and refresh yourselves, rest from your weariness. Our water is your water. I can't speak for turnips and blood..." (here he broke into a wide smile) "...but, by the grace of God, water is abundant here in this spot—a true miracle from the Blessed Mother. You will find that we are rich, therefore; rich with fruitful crops and numerous sheep and goats."

Hans had skulked up during this interchange and he whispered to in my ear in the Dutch-based Afrikaner language. "Baas, remember the story of the spider and the fly. This is a pretty mirage complete with four smiling spiders."

Really, I was becoming impatient with his ceaseless negativity, but I said, "And what do you propose I do, be still more rude and refuse their hospitality? Besides, we are grown men and well armed and we will be able to protect ourselves if there is trouble."

"Baas, you are no doubt right and far be it from me to suspect your judgment, but still a little voice inside me worries that our gateway to the Big Baas's house in the sky may be through the belly of a cannibal." At this point I chose to ignore my servant, whose protestations had attracted the curiosity of our hosts. I sidestepped the issue by happily accepting the invitation to enter and refresh ourselves.

The priests turned and entered their grounds, and we all gratefully followed, though I must admit that a verse from the Scriptures popped into my brain at that moment, "Enter ye in at the strait gate: For wide is the gate, and broad is the way, that leadeth to destruction . . . ."

In any event, of course, having no foreknowledge of the astonishing things that would befall us, we entered and found that the rosery included a most delightful well, from which we drank our fill of clean, fresh water. Thus we rested for awhile longer in that wonderful little garden with the fragrance of roses filling the air.

Once situated thus, I noticed that the monastery structure was actually two structures. The building to the left as we faced them was the smaller and was in fact the priests' living quarters. The larger, on the right, was the chapel, or church.

Eventually we were led into the former and shown into a large functional room where we gratefully doffed our kits and sat on the crude benches that surrounded an equally crude table.

I asked: "Sir, when was this church constructed? It seems so odd to have a church isolated so, in the middle of the desert."

"As a matter of fact, construction began in the year 1500—a nice round year, don't you think? Our order is one that sought isolation, the better to meditate and seek revelations from God—away from the distractions of the world."

Huxley spoke: "My good man, if that is the case, we are sorry that we have arrived on the scene and disrupted your meditative way of life."

"Think nothing of it. We also consider ourselves a holy oasis for weary travelers. Though, of course, we have few enough of those!"

"Tabot," I inquired. "You said that you were informed of our arrival. By whom?"

"Oh! By the Afar—or the Danakil, as they are known outside this land, but 'Afar' is what they call themselves. They have been monitoring your movements since your ship arrived at Annesley Bay. A hardy but terribly mean-spirited people, as I'm afraid you have found out the hard way. They had promised us that they would leave you undisturbed, but I suppose the temptation to raid and perhaps acquire a few trophies..." here he couldn't help but smile sardonically; later he explained that Afar men, to prove their manhood, collected their enemies' testicles, which they dried and hung from a large curved blade that each warrior wears forever across his stomach "...was more than they could bear."

"I suppose entertainment options are limited here," Huxley muttered.

"We regret their behavior terribly and apologize most profusely," Tabot went on. "I am glad that there was no loss of life among your party." Then he hesitated. "I fear for your friend Cuff, though."

Henry Stanley ventured a question at that time. "Tabot, how do you and your priest colleagues manage to avoid becoming, yourselves, souvenirs of your spies?"

"For centuries there has been an agreement, a time-honored agreement. They serve as our eyes and ears and we pave the way for them to a higher world, as we have touched some of them a bit with matters of the spirit. But, I'm afraid that this breach in our agreement causes us some concern. My brothers and I will deliberate on that and decide how we will respond." Whereupon he left us to ourselves for a time.

Tabot eventually returned and told us we were to tour the chapel, or church, and suddenly all of my charges rose at once and all but marched after the priest, with Hans, Bayushtiak, and myself following.

The church was circular, and in a moment we found ourselves on a walkway that circled it. This walkway was open at the sides but covered by an awning of thatch. Tabot walked us around this path explaining that he and his brother priests used this area in particular to sing hymns to God as they walked in endless circles around the building. We came to an opening in the outside wall and entered. For a brief moment I became disoriented. It was as though I had stepped into an art gallery of the British Museum. This was an enclosed inner circuit or walkway (the *k'ane mahlet*), which in turn circled a further interior chamber. What had taken me aback was that the walls of the *k'ane mahlet* were literally covered with paintings of the Virgin Mary in every conceivable pose. There she was alone in the desert, alone in the jungle, surrounded by handmaidens in the desert, surrounded by handmaidens in the jungle, adored in the city, adored by animals, bathing under waterfalls, with the baby Jesus and without, with angels and without, clothed and unclothed.

Stanley leaned in to examine a couple and he exclaimed, "Damn, these could be Leonardos!" But then he moved on to take in more riches.

One painting in particular captured the attention of Richard Holmes. I was standing next to him, so I can relate that as he began gazing at the painting with great interest, he started and gasped. His attention was riveted to the piece. He leaned over and examined it and whispered, "My God, Quatermain, look where she is standing!" I observed that the artist had chosen to place his Mary in the middle of what was obviously a large and luxuriously appointed library, but one that housed scrolls rather than books. These scrolls were piled in cubbies of which there were three or four dozen or so visible in the background.

Holmes's excitement, of course, drew all the others closer and each of them in turn became excited at the genius so evident in the piece—a piece hanging on a wall in an unknown monastery in the middle of an awful desert in a country that Europeans for the most part were barely aware of.

Holmes turned to Tabot. "Please, can you tell me the provenance of these paintings, and in particular this one." Tabot hesitated. It seemed he was taken off guard by the question. "Please forgive me if I don't have an immediate response. We do, you understand, live with these renderings every day and don't often think about their origins, merely grateful that we have been chosen by God to be their caretakers."

He paused to reflect for a few moments, then continued. "This church was constructed in the year 1500. As soon as it was completed, all the Christian churches of Ethiopia and, in particular, one of the churches in Axum, St. Mary of Zion far to the north, presented to us, or to this chapel, much of this collection for the glory of Jesus and of his mother, Mariam, daughter of God. The remainder have made their way here over the years, as our existence is not unknown to the other orthodox churches of the land."

Holmes was persistent, however. "This painting showing a collection of scrolls, I was wondering what could have been the model."

Tabot hesitated for the briefest of moments, then shrugged. "No doubt it was inspired by God in the highest."

"I'm sure," muttered Holmes.

Certainly all these paintings triggered a number of thoughts and emotions in the various members of my party, but the upshot of it was that we were still in the dark as much as before.

In any event, we elected to continue our little tour of the church. We came to another opening—this one in the innermost wall of the *k'ane mahlet*—and entered yet another interior chamber. This proved to be still another walkway surrounding yet another interior chamber. This walkway was called the *keddest*, which Tabot explained was a place dedicated to prayer and communion. The central chamber beyond we learned was called the *mak'das*, and it was there that the Holy of Holies was located.

The Holy of Holies was exactly what it sounds like. Only the most senior priests ever could enter the area. This is where something immensely holy called *tabots* were kept. I couldn't help but note the similarity to our host's name, but Tabot avoided answering my questions and it was only after subsequent determined effort that I got him to explain that he was named after the *tabots*, and that they were replicas of the tablets God presented to Moses—that is to say, the stone tablets on which God wrote the Ten Commandments. He also explained that every Ethiopian church was constructed in the same manner, and it had been so since time immemorial—the most holy tabots housed within a central Holy of Holies surrounded by concentric circular walkways, so that if seen from above, the whole arrangement would look like a target with the Holy of Holies as the bull's-eye.

We wound back around through the circuits and exited the church and soon were back at the large room we had been provided when we first entered. As soon as we were left alone, we jumped at the chance to compare notes, to theorize, and the like. I even caught sight of Hans and Bayushtiak off in a corner speaking quietly between themselves (Hans seldom deigned to share his opinions with anyone but me).

In due course, a simple but filling meal made up of honey-sweetened flat bread, onions, and goat's milk cheese was brought in, and eventually we tired of talk and rested for the duration of the night. Cuff, in the meantime, was still being tended to, or nursed, by the priests in an area reserved for such medical requirements.

The next morning, after we had freshened ourselves, a messenger arrived saying that Tabot wanted to see us immediately. In time, we had congregated outside in the rosery since our group was rather large and all the rooms large enough to accommodate us were in use by the monks and priests.

Tabot arrived and greeted us. Then he said the most extraordinary things. "Gentlemen and my lady," he began. "While the Afar had alerted us to your coming and while we are bound to aid you as necessary, to be frank, your presence here—especially the number of you—is creating a larger problem than expected, as it imposes on our way of life. Last night I prayed upon the problem and in a dream three angels came to me in the form of the Three Kings. Gaspar was the head angel in the dream and he said that my guests were very special and that I should ask them (that is to say, you) for a token, simple as it may be, and that if you had the correct token, then you were to be escorted into the presence of the Holy Mother herself, which is a very rare honor indeed." As you can imagine, at the mention of the name Gaspar, Holmes's and my eyes locked meaningfully.

Someone, I think it was Stanley, asked what he meant by a "token" and also, in an uncharacteristically rude fashion, to my mind, what he meant by "escorted into the presence of the Holy Mother," and just who was she?

Unperturbed, Tabot responded, "Why, the token is the key by which you will see the Holy Mother, and the Holy Mother is the mother of God, of course, and you will see her because it is her wish, should you have the token. Are there any more questions?" And then he waited.

Hans whispered about then, "Baas, what is this? It was so simple before—hello and good-bye, have some food, rest awhile, but now he is talking about a holy sign, which is different. Even your Predikant father wouldn't talk the way that this priest with a face like granite is doing. And certainly I would rather not see any Holy Mother for fear she might be real."

I for one wasn't concerned whether this mysterious mother was real or not. I was more concerned that it sounded suspiciously as though we were about to be taken somewhere against our own free will. I was about to say as much when the priest held out his hand palm up. This was enough to quiet me.

We all started looking at one another muttering, "A token, what could be a token?" I was thinking that it could be just about anything, from one of Miss Mitchell's hair combs to the cork from Hans's beloved square-face that he liked to sniff and that he kept in lieu of the actual bottle, when that self-same Miss Mitchell inquired, "Perhaps your angels were referring to one of my rocks from the sky?" Tabot merely continued to stand with his hand out. She then inquired in an impatient tone, "Well then, can you please give us an idea of what we are supposed to show you?" Tabot was still silent.

Then Peachy Carnehan spoke, "Say, Huxley, I have a notion. More 'an likely what he's lookin' for is something out of the ordinary. Anyone could show a bullet or, say, a compass or handkerchief. What about one of those remarkable bits of bone you found out there in the desert by that cave. Give that a try."

Frowning, Thomas Huxley then unpacked some of the rolls of cotton he had used to store his fossils and unrolled one very carefully. In due course, a finger bone became visible and it was shown to Tabot, who bent forward to peer at the bone. Then he grinned and turned smartly around and started walking away from us through the rose bushes, heading

"...the priest held out his hand, palm up."

toward the entrance of the wall that surrounded the church. When he got there, he motioned for us to follow.

Hans and I looked at one another and shrugged. It appeared that the bone was the key, though at the time I could not fathom why. Later on, I realized that it made sense.

We were soon escorted once more to the open walkway that surrounded the church and where the priests even then were walking in endless circles around the perimeter of the church. From there we were taken into the *k'ane mahlet* where we had seen all the beautiful Madonna paintings housed. It was here that I first became aware of an extremely pungent incense (that later I was to learn was frankincense) and from there into the inner communion circuit, the *keddest*. In the *keddest*, Tabot paused and waited till he had all our attentions.

He pointed to a curtain that clearly entered into another chamber. "This," he said, "is as far as any uninitiated has ever gotten, for beyond this is the *mak'das*, the Holy of Holies where the *tabots* rest, the tablets of Moses." At this moment, several more priests joined us, and Tabot very dramatically and deliberately thrust aside the curtain and bade us enter. I wish I could tell you with some certainty what I saw in that small chamber, but in fact, the incense was so heavy that vision was impaired. Having been told several times that this was the Holy of Holies itself where the *tabots* were kept, I strained to get a glimpse of the sacred objects or their container, but I could see nothing. Whether they were obscured or even removed I never learned. When we were all inside, Tabot motioned to one of the priests who pushed aside another curtain revealing a space no larger than a closet. The priest then pulled aside the rug that was there, thus revealing a wooden door in the floor, which door proved to be heavy if the man's struggles to open it were warranted.

This, in turn, exposed stairs leading down. Some of us expressed considerable concern about what this was all about, but we nonetheless let ourselves be led docilely down the stairs, through a short tunnel and then up again, where we emerged into a sort of cave.

That cave opened into what I immediately understood was a cleft in the cliff wall beside which the church had been built. I was already familiar with something of the sort since the horrible Black Kloof, the home of Zikali, "The Opener of Roads," was entered by way of a similar breach in the face of a precipice.

Light poured down from the sun above into what would have appeared to be a crevasse from above, and a well-worn earth path lay before us.

With Tabot leading the way, we explorers marched forward. We rounded a bend in the path, and the wall suddenly flowered with decorative murals—paintings, carvings, and friezes—depicting various aspects of the Madonna in similar poses to those we had seen in the *k'ane mahlet.*

Holmes was again and quickly beside himself with ecstasy. He reached out to touch one of the figures. But before his hand had moved a foot in the direction of the wall, one of the priests had quickly moved and grabbed his elbow. The normally congenial-appearing priest suddenly wore an ugly scowl, startling Holmes and myself—for I was next to Holmes and was able to observe the priest's expression—so that we both caught our breath. The man's visage was positively horrific!

Thus warned off, we proceeded along the path keeping our hands to ourselves. For perhaps half an hour we moved along the path. Sometimes it was extremely narrow so that we could only progress by removing our kits and sidling alongside-wise. Hans, Miss Mitchell, Carnehan and myself had no problem, being either small or thin in stature. Stanley, Huxley, Holmes, Dravot, and Bayushtiak found these intervals rather tight going. Other times the path opened up so that the distance between vertical walls might have been as much as ten yards. Above, I was happy to see that the sky still shown clearly through the crevasse.

I couldn't help but wonder what our fates would be if an earthquake happened to hit just then. Would the walls move in and flatten us, or would they come crumbling down—with the same effect but from a different direction?

Finally, we saw light ahead of us and I could see that we were approaching the end of the crack in the plateau. A moment later I saw that it opened up into a kind of wide gorge. A bit more and I stepped into the open and I was so overwhelmed with images that I hardly know where to begin describing them.

Totally unexpectedly I saw a crowd of people, perhaps thirty in number, dressed as from another era—my first thought was of Biblical times. Women mainly, with some men and children, most wearing brightly colored striped robes or ankle-length skirts. They were standing, talking or strolling in a kind of village square with a pool and fountain in the center. From the center of the pool rose a statue of a young woman with a great jar in her arms, and from the jar water poured into the pool, splashing noisily. There was something joy-filled and mysterious about the statue and something else, too, but all this was quickly swept from my mind as events unfolded.

Beyond the square, I saw a compact community with connected buildings built of stone. From our vantage point, we could see a main thoroughfare made of rough flagstones held together with mortar leading from the square down, around, and past countless functional stone edifices until it disappeared into the distance.

All this I saw in an instant, and the next instant, the normal harmony of the place was disturbed as you would expect when the priests from the cleft appeared with a large clutch of strangers of varied appearances.

A woman with authority in her bearing was approaching us. She walked right up to Tabot and they spoke, using what I assumed was the region's Coptic tongue. She was perhaps middle aged, with a cragged but thoroughly noble face. Over her head—which I could see was crowned with the richest of chestnut colored hair—she wore a loosely fitting covering of the deepest blue. The overall effect was quite wonderful. She had been sitting on the edge of the pool in quiet discussion with a group of other younger women when her attention had been drawn to the passage opening where we emerged.

This woman and Tabot had stepped aside some distance and continued to confer. There was much gesticulation with their faces turning in our direction numerous times and all manner of other signs to indicate that our sudden appearance was not altogether welcome.

Eventually they both approached us—or rather me. The priest introduced the woman as Ruth, who was a teacher, and told us that the roles of himself and his fellow priests had been satisfied according to the laws of the matter that had been set down more than four centuries before at the time the church had been established. And without further ado, that whole bunch turned and returned the way we had come, and we wouldn't see them again for some time.

Ruth then faced me and spoke. Her language was quite incomprehensible to any of us, even to the inexhaustible Stanley. Then approaching it rather academically, Holmes and Stanley conferred between themselves and decided it must be a form of Coyne, the ancient popular form of Greek that long since had faded from the planet. In lieu of using her language, between us we tried English, French, Zulu, Dutch (that is to say Afrikaans), and several others to no avail, all to the clear frustration of all involved.

There came a moment when all the reasonable options seemed to have been used up, and we sunk into a long silence, our collective mood being that of defeat.

Then Stanley snapped his fingers! Facing Ruth, he launched into another language that was vaguely familiar to me. Suddenly Ruth's face lit up. She took Stanley by the hand and took him aside where they whispered together and it was perfectly clear that they were in fact communicating quite well.

When they returned to our group, Stanley was grinning ear to ear. "I had a hunch is all," he said. "I've been wondering about those anomalous Leonardos in the chapel." This time Ruth addressed our group again while focusing on Stanley. She opened her mouth and out emerged a slow and guttural, yet perfectly recognizable (so Stanley affirmed) and passable Italian! Then Holmes himself made inquiries in the modern form of the language, which he had a passing knowledge of, and, eventually, a sort of general conversation was established.

During this interlude, one of the first questions put to her, by me, if I recall correctly, through Stanley, was "Why is it that she spoke Italian?"

She replied that centuries before, they had been visited by two great men who spoke in this manner and these men had tarried among them for months and spent some of that time sharing their language. Even after they left, by instruction from the Holy Mother—who at the time I took to be some sort of priestess—Ruth's people had handed the language down from novice to novice in preparation for the great day when it would be needed again. In fact, she was extremely disappointed in herself for not immediately recalling the age-old writ that required her people to use the Tongue of the Messengers, as she called it, when confronted by strangers. That we were the first such strangers in some 400 years did not seem to matter!

Nonetheless, she seemed to quickly get over her lapse, then gestured at us in our well-traveled and unfamiliar clothes and giggled. Holmes extracted from her that in her mind's eye she had always envisioned that if she ever needed to use the Tongue of the Messengers in her lifetime, it would be to individuals resembling the great prophets, not to a ragtag group of heathens!

We Europeans smiled at this and I asked Stanley to convey our gratitude and other various courtesies that I had learned over the years after much travel were always well regarded regardless of the culture or level of civilization.

She accepted the compliments and bowed slightly, gesturing with her arm to follow her. It was at this point that Hans, who had been unnaturally quiet during this whole interchange, chose to speak, this time in Dutch.

"Baas! Mayhap I have been thinking that we are even now within a great hole in the rock, a hole much like the holes made by worms in apples, and just as the worm is in the power of the great beast that presses the apple within its jaws, we are likely to be flattened if the rocks come tumbling down or if the crowds choose to rise up."

"Old fool!" was my response. "Do you think I have not thought of these things? But what can we do? We are here now, and do I need remind you that we are here largely because of your proddings yonder, back in Durban? Nevertheless, though this is all very strange, in its own way it is wondrous and I for one am interested to know what happens next."

Hans appeared to be somewhat chastened by my retort, though, as usual, he needed to have the final word: "Ah, Baas, that may be so, but please don't forget that an apple infested with worms is a rotten apple!"

I suppose I must have looked at him particularly fiercely for he turned on his heels and I lost sight of him, though, of course, I knew in my heart that drunk or sober, angry or not, he would never be far from my side.

Ruth motioned for us to follow her. She took us through the throng of people, who parted before us, chattering, much as I suppose the waters parted before Moses. She led us out of the town square and onto the road (which was the only one I ever noted aside from a few paths). This road was bounded on both sides as far as one could see with buildings, that is to say dwellings, and as we passed I saw many women and children poking their heads out of the small windows or watching us from the roofs. These were one-story structures made of slabs of rock mortared together. Doors were not prominent I noticed but I saw that between every two or three houses there was a narrow alley, which led me to believe that the doors were on the side of the house opposite the street, that is to say in the backs of the houses, which I learned later was a correct assumption.

We walked thus down the main road, which twisted and turned down the middle of what amounted to a great gorge cut through the mountain, for perhaps somewhat more than a mile. Though the gorge was clearly mostly of natural design, there were many indications that certain areas were enlarged or shaped by the hand of man. Perhaps such areas were the quarries from which the town's people acquired their housing materials. I never did ask. Accompanying us the whole length were the homes and structures that made up the village, or perhaps town would be a better word, and of course most of the population, which we learned comprised some two thousand individuals, turned out to get the best view of us.

At the end of the road, Ruth finally stopped before a temple-like structure that was built on a gentle slope so that it rose in tiered gardens up from the street. I could see through the gate and beyond and saw that encircling the structure was a small courtyard comprising still more gardens with convenient stone benches to rest upon, not unlike the monastery rosery that had so affected poor Cuff. However, Ruth bade us not to enter the interior.

Instead, she asked us to follow her a bit more and she took us a little distance off to the right and up a ramp to a separate building, which proved to be a sort of community building. We were led into an open central court, where we were met by attendants who took charge of us as Ruth went her own way and disappeared. The robed attendants led us to rooms that were distributed among us as follows: Hans and I shared one room, Holmes and Huxley another, and Bayushtiak and Miss Mitchell were each allocated a room to themselves, and Stanley and the two soldiers shared another. In addition we were shown where we could bathe.

Not that this distribution really mattered at all, for as soon as we were left alone, we all gathered in one of the rooms, that of Stanley and the soldiers, as it was somewhat larger than the others, to discuss this totally unexpected turn of events.

Oh! Ruth at some point in our tour of the gorge told us the name of the community as we followed her, we learned that this community—hidden away behind the Holy of Holies of the Chapel of the Immaculate Heart and secreted within a great chasm visible only to the birds in the sky—bore the name *Sinai*.

✿ ✿ ✿

You can imagine our riot of talking when finally we were alone. Stanley was certain we had discovered a hidden city of Hebrews who had been cut off from advancing civilization perhaps two thousand years ago. He and Holmes discussed and argued about these people's language, their architecture, their manner of dress, where they could have obtained the bright dyes and materials for their clothes, and any other detail that entered their minds. There were, however, two observations that troubled them deeply. They could not understand the apparent matriarchal tenor of the culture—whereas Hebrews were supposed to be typically and steadfastly patriarchal. Also, they were baffled by the presence of a statue of a young woman in the village square. Old-time Hebrews, they said, would not have—indeed, *could* not have—allowed such a "graven image" in their midst.

Finally, in the evening, a messenger came and bade us follow her, and we were all escorted to a hall in the council building. We had no choice but to stand as there was no place to sit in the spare surroundings. In time, there came the low throbbing of a bell, ringing over and over again. After nearly fifty interminable rings, it ceased and a procession of thirteen women, one of whom was Ruth, marched in—or to be more accurate, twelve women and a girl, and the girl was being held aloft in a kind of litter carried by half of the women. The procession was well practiced and I felt I was watching a performance at the theater or even one of the well-choreographed ceremonies of the Zulu kings.

The women who were not carrying the litter moved to positions around a kind of raised dais. The others set the litter gently before the ramp that led to the dais, then joined their sisters and arranged themselves in the manner of a royal guard. The girl moved quickly up to the bench, sat primly down, turned, and looked out over us all. The entire retinue turned to face the girl with looks of obvious reverence and a great hush fell over the hall. The girl continued to look at us curiously for a time, and I tried to spot some sort of shyness or nervousness as you would expect to see in a young girl in similar circumstances, but in vain for she seemed totally poised.

When she had her fill of looking at us, she stood up and we were able to get our first really good look at her. I could hardly believe it: there was before us just a bit of a girl barely four feet tall with a complexion like fresh cream, standing quite calmly. She wore a simple white cloth robe with a belt of golden fabric, and over her shoulders was a blue shawl. I could see ringlets of black lustrous hair falling from under the white scarf-like cloth, or veil, that covered her head. In her hands she held an arrangement of roses of every color, the fragrance of which I perceived even though we were some distance from her. There were also yellow roses attached to her feet somehow perhaps with a ribbon. Was she some sort of leader? I thought of Tibet's Dalai Lama who, I had heard, always began his rule as a child.

Our group stood respectfully before and below her. Then she opened her mouth and spoke. And the voice that emerged from her mouth was the purest most crystalline expression of a human voice that I had ever heard.

The voice was a girl's to be sure, but it was also a woman's. It sounded as though it came from above and beyond the firmament and from below our feet from some sort of vast hidden cavern at the same time. It sounded like all these things at once, and what it said was, "My good people, thank you for coming" in English! "I have been expecting you for quite sometime."

The girl smiled at each of us and her smile was truly like sunlight radiating upon us. "I am Mariam," she said. Then she gestured around her saying, "And these are my people. I have brought you all here to Sinai from your far off homes for my purposes, as I have secret and holy tasks for each of you [hearing this, several of us looked quizzically at one another with raised eyebrows]. However, with one of your party I will share, and through him to the rest of the world, knowledge of the holiest place on earth! I say again, the holiest place on earth!

"Long have men sought treasures such as the cup from which they believed Christ drank, or the Ark of the Covenant, or for the true mountain called Sinai, or fragments from my son's tree, and so much more.

"Well, I, of all people, know well what is holy and what is not and what is more holy or less holy, for I am the mother of God, and you have come to this remote spot at my bidding though you knew it not. You, each of you, came now rather than before or later because the time is soon coming when the people of this world must learn the truth of their own existence."

Here she paused, probably aware that her each and every utterance was potent, ripe with astonishing concepts, and pregnant with controversy. My impression was that she stopped to allow us to take in and digest the vastness of her brief speech. In a minute, she continued.

"They say that God created man in His own image. There is truth to that, not in the material sense, for the material aspect of God can be better thought of as the entire world on which we stand, and, by extension, perhaps the Universe without as well. No, man is created in God's image in the sense of 'mind' and spirit. Of all the creatures on earth, man is the only one that can seek God consciously, or who can arrive at God's door through attainment of merit, for God created man to join with and become God—and the destiny of each man, woman, and child is to attain God, whether he knows it or not, wants it or not, needs it or not. And though some men may not consciously strive for this, in time they will arrive there in any case.

"Have you never gone back to the spot of your birth and wondered at the fact that it was there in that precise midwife's home or there in that very room or there in that exact glade that you came into existence, where you were born into this world? Now I bid you think. At such moments, are you not full of wonder for your very existence, for the miracle of your life?"

Her pause this time seemed especially prolonged. Then she said, "Well, I have brought you here to make it clear that mankind likewise has a place where it came into existence, where it was born, and it is time that all of mankind learn of that place so that all may feel that self-same wonder.

"The Holy Scriptures tell of the creation of the world and a place that is called Eden…" Suddenly the girl sagged, and Ruth and some of the other women jumped to her aid in a practiced manner and helped her sit back down on the dais. The girl became quiet as the women fussed over her, and I think we all used the opportunity to reflect further on what we had just heard.

When the girl regained some of her strength, she whispered to Ruth, who clearly wanted Mariam to return to the litter, but she held fast and got a set expression on her face. Her attendants moved away and stood at reverent attention as they had before. Mariam faced us again and continued in her mystical voice.

"But first, before I discuss the realm that is the real Eden of the real world, you need to know more of myself. There is skepticism among you, and that is good, for what good would you be as my messengers if you were to believe all that you heard from whomever you heard it. So I will explain somewhat. As all the world knows well, Jesus asked his beloved disciple to care for his mother. That person is myself."

It was, unexpectedly, Carnehan who first reacted to this preposterous announcement. "God A'mighty! Just how are we supposed to believe that! I've heard some bloomin' tall tales in my life—" Also, unexpectedly, it was a glare from Bayushtiak that stopped him in mid-sentence.

Mariam continued as though nothing had happened. "Thus, John and I headed north and resided in Ephaesus in Turkey for a time. However, we chose to continue our journey north and settled in what is now the countries you call France and England, but that did not suit our purposes either. We continued our search for a permanent home and then returned south. When we eventually came to this land, which was far more green and fertile two thousand years ago, the angel Gabriel came to me as he had before and declared that our journeying was finished and that this spot was to be our home. He split asunder the rock cliff, creating this hidden valley, and bade John and me enter.

"'Verily,'" he said, "'this spot where I have brought you is holy,' he said, 'more so than Ur was where the Lord spoke to Abraham or the Mountain of

Sinai where the Lord spoke to Moses. Though these are surely holy places, the spot I show you is holier still, for it is the holiest spot on earth. And verily, you who are the Mother of God, you are bid to attend this veritable womb of mankind, for are you not the holiest person of the world? Thus, is it not right that you should live by and in and protect the holiest place? Are you not also the mother of man? Then it is fitting that you reside by and in and protect the womb of man. Verily, I say to you, this spot is the most holy in the eyes and mind of God.'"

"And then the angel caused me to see through his eyes. He showed me a vast valley that ran the whole length of this land from north to south, a tremendous valley with many lakes. The angel bade John and I settle in this very spot that is under our feet now, which is the northernmost gateway both into and out of the great valley. Over the years, mainly by sending dispatches to Galilee, we gathered around ourselves the people who were to become our community.

"I was ninety-seven years old when the great miracle happened. Death came to claim me as it does everyone, and, Lo!, Gabriel was there for me one more time. He told me that our Father wished me to tarry for there was more for me to do on Earth. Thus, at the point of my bodily death my spirit entered the body of a certain twelve-year-old girl and that child became Mariam for a year, that is, my soul, my personality, all that is invisible that was Mariam the mother of Jesus entered that girl and the girl became me. Following that, every year the woman who was Mariam moved from twelve-year-old to twelve-year-old so that the Mother of God is nearly always within the body of a living girl. Through the mind and bodies of these girls, I have lived on."

Here, Ruth interjected: "The blessed Mother of God lives on eternally!" The girl paused again then, and I dared to break the mood by asking a question. "If what you say is true, why does the Virgin, that is you, trouble twelve year olds?"

Mariam looked at Ruth, who responded for her, "Because that was the age of Mariam when the Angel of the Lord came to her and revealed to her that she would in time to come conceive Jesus through the Holy Spirit, for in those days, and still in our land, that is the age of promise for a girl."

Some of our party looked at one another in dismay at this statement. It was Stanley who merely shrugged and reminded us that cultures the world over have different standards.

As Mariam sat quietly gazing over us, Ruth then went into more detail concerning the "possession" of the girls. In brief what she explained is

"…that is the age of promise for a girl."

as follows: when a girl ceases to be Mariam, she has no memory of that whole year. It is as though she made the transition from eleven to thirteen with no year between. Sometimes it happened that, when it was time for Mariam to move out of her body, there was no twelve-year old girl to act as her vessel.

It is at those times, as Mariam waits for an eleven-year-old to come of age, that she appears as an apparition in various places around the world for a little time, Guadalupe, Mexico, for one, and more recently in La Salette and Lourdes, both in France, where she shared some of her insights with some chosen children or others in whom innocence abounded.

Naturally, Ruth went on, there are all sorts of ceremonies built up around the miracle, with parents vying for their daughters to be "the One." The only time when it is guaranteed that a particular girl becomes Mariam is when there is only one twelve-year old girl in the town.

Then Ruth went a bit more into the history of the place: in the 4th century, when the Library of Alexandria was threatened, many of its greatest volumes were secretly shipped to this community, since its existence and location were known to the great librarians of the time. Thus, the town of Sinai held close to its bosom the wisdom of millennia. Then, centuries later, another miracle happened, which Stanley had guessed. For in the "fullness of time" two men stumbled out of the desert into their gorge, teaching the language of the messengers while they tarried.

Then all at once, the girl's posture slumped and her eyes rolled back. At that her entire retinue, including Ruth, went into motion, swooping her into the litter and hurrying her into another room.

Ruth returned quickly to explain that our interview would continue another day, and then she led us some distance to a dining room where we were treated as honored guests, and we enjoyed more of the simple fare of these people.

Afterward, we were taken again to our rooms. For some peculiar reason, we did not converse much when left to ourselves. It was as though we were all spiritually fatigued. I do remember that Holmes was irate about something and that Huxley was particularly subdued.

Frankly I cared little about anything just then. I was confused. Nothing I had heard had made any sense, though I could not deny the sincerity of these people. I lay down with my sleeping roll, and the last thing I remembered was that Hans was curled up next to me snoring.

The following morning our meal consisted of cakes and honey, apples, and raisins, with cool goat's milk to quench our thirst. The woman we had come to know as the messenger came and indicated that I was to follow her. All the others were to stay behind. She took me through a veritable labyrinth of passages when finally she stopped and indicated that we were to enter a particular room and wait.

The room was Spartan as all things were in this land. These people did not seem to have much heart for decorating or for jewelry, bangles, and the like. I did as she bade, making myself as comfortable as I could on some cushions that were on the floor. About twenty minutes later Ruth and some other women entered solemnly, walking slowly. Once again, in the middle of this procession was Mariam, walking this time on her own power. She came to a simple enough chair and sat facing me, her matrons standing in an arc behind her.

"Allan, I have asked to see you now because, of your party, you alone are destined to live through the ages, not as I who do so here secretly in the desert, but in the minds of men for all time . . . as I survive in the hearts of men who know not my real situation. I wished to see you in order to finish what I began to say yesterday."

Here I had to protest. "But what about Mr. Huxley and Mr. Stanley and Miss Mitchell? Surely they are, all three, far greater than I and—"

"Yes, Allan, in an ideal world, Maria Mitchell, Henry Stanley, and Richard Holmes should and would enjoy renown through all time, but the people of earth have short memories or are fickle and, sad to say, the time is not far off when those names will be lost, save for those few historians and practitioners in their fields who may remember. Now listen carefully, for one asset I do not have is strength.

"The Holy Scriptures tell of the creation of the world . . . and they tell of God creating man in the land of Eden and that the act of creation took mere moments. These statements are of course true, but who is to determine what is a moment in the eyes of God, who measures time in billions of years? Indeed, God created man in a moment, a mere few million years, and he did this feat in a place that you can call Eden for want of a better name. I have brought you here to identify that real place to you and thus to all men.

"O, Allan, let me tell you a wonderful truth. Remember, thee, how the Lord through the burning bush told Moses that he stood on holy ground? Well I say to you that the ground on which you stand is holier still." As she said this last, her eyes grew large and she smiled for the first time, as though savoring her words.

"I am growing weak, for the girl who is my vessel was never strong, but I must share with you the secret that makes this place so holy. That spot, which is under your feet, continues south, making up the great valley of eastern Africa, the bowl out of which sprang man, the crucible where the embryonic spirit, or God-in-the-making called mankind, was forged."

Just then, some women emerged from a door carrying great censers dangling from golden chains and filled with burning incense. Great clouds of the stuff very quickly filled the room and suddenly, I felt as though I had been absorbed into a dream. But just before I went under, I suddenly understood. Like a bright light, it came to me. The girl, albeit very small and very young, was just another wizard of the Zikali ilk! Just another Old Cheat with more of that horrid magical smoke!

The gist of the dream was that I became a witness to the shifting geographies of the prehistoric earth and watched vast forests and jungles and deserts ebb and flow, and I saw the migrations of a myriad animal species and watched them alter their forms to better survive in their constantly changing habitats, or go extinct. Eventually, my attention was made to focus on the family of apes, and I saw the trials and tribulations they experienced through the millennia, and how they adapted, and how there came a time when some of them rose up on their own two feet and walked, following which their ability to command their environments gained momentum—

I then slowly came out of a deep sleep and regaining awareness of my surroundings—of the slim twelve-year-old girl before me.

By degrees I regained my composure. Then a thought came to me. "But it was only a dream, nothing concrete, nothing at all but smoke." I paused then said, "Dear Lady, that was quite a trick. Yet, how can I trust what I have seen and heard?"

"That is a matter of choice," replied the girl. "You may trust or not trust as you desire. I can only remind you that I brought you here from far-off to show you that which you have now seen. My purpose was to share the truth of man's origin with him most able to divine it and appreciate its meaning. After all, we"—and here she made an all-encompassing sweep of her arms—"are all the children of God, and God wants his children to grow beyond the quaint stories they tell amongst themselves and to hearken to things as they really are.

"I did this in the only manner I can. What you choose to think of it, that I cannot help. For my part, I am only showing you the earth's most divine

truth. All of what you witnessed happened right here and yonder as well."
Here she indicated south.

"Listen to me now!"

At this point, her normal ethereal, but nonetheless calm, voice changed, indeed, her whole demeanor suddenly took on a fiery passion.

"If God is as real as, for instance, me, and is by definition divine, and if through the use of the tool called Time, he crafted people in his own image, then it would follow that people are also divine and that the spot where He did his crafting must be holy ground—the holiest of ground.

"I have drawn you here from afar to tell you my wishes. During my incarnations in Guadeloupe, Lourdes, Fatima, and such, I have asked, or otherwise let it be known, only two things of consequence. First, that all mankind turn away from sin, chiefly your disregard for God and, too, the lust for war. Second, that a chapel be built on the spot of my appearance in my honor. Well, now I ask something similar of you. I ask that all the terrain from where you stand to the southernmost reach of the great valley—the vast bowl that is birthplace of the human race—be designated holy ground and be set aside so all people can come and contemplate their existence, to perceive with their own eyes the spot where God's greatest miracle occurred, and this will make them more mindful of one another and of God, as well."

I couldn't help but interject here. "Excuse me, miss, but are you saying that you drew me from Durban and perhaps the others as well, and that you did this with powers unknown to us, for the sole purpose of telling me that you want this barren desert and lands beyond turned into a place of worship?"

"Yes, a natural cathedral."

Her words struck me dumb. Finally I was able to gather the resources to say, "My dear lady, what you are asking is preposterous. What you have described is perhaps one-fifth of the African continent, making up the national territories of numerous nations. Even if every leader of every one of those countries could see the same vision I have been graced with, there is no way they could all agree to turn large parts of their countries into contiguous reserves for your so-called holy ground, or whatever you want to call it."

Mariam did not deign to comment, nor change her expression from the beatific smile that she seemed to wear forever. She merely gestured to her hand maidens and prepared to leave. However, just as she was about to disappear behind a curtain, she stopped and turned and said, "Allan, rest assured that in the fullness of time all these things are possible and will be fulfilled! For you are my tool and, therefore, blessed by God!"

Then she was gone.

I returned to my room in a daze. The entire interview from beginning to end was outrageous, and I felt insulted that the inhabitants of this valley would assume that I would swallow any part of this pretense. They actually thought I would believe we'd been interviewed by the Virgin Mary Mother of God. Then to make matters worse, they drugged me with some toxic substance and wanted me to believe the further nonsense that there had once been a totally unknown and new upright ape that mankind was related to. And finally, the last straw, so to speak, was this astonishing attempt to reveal their desire to turn one-fifth of Africa into some sort of continental preserve.

I could not discuss any of this with the others of our expedition, much to their chagrin. They tried, nonetheless, to draw me out, but I would have none of it, and the day ended quietly enough.

The next morning, the messenger came and fetched Richard Holmes, who, it turned out would be gone for days. We were all concerned about this but were continually reassured that he was well, and that, in fact, he was probably never better.

It was during this interval that Cuff passed from us. The priests kindly sent word to us from the chapel. They said there was nothing more they could have done for him except make him comfortable. At this news, some of us remembered his principal passion in life and then put our heads together. We sent back a message asking if Cuff could be laid to rest in a corner of that rosery, or rose garden, he had taken such a shine to. The priests, who had, for some days, patiently weathered the brunt of his delirium and his preoccupation with their garden, said they understood and agreed.

They buried him with ceremony, or so we understood, as we were a long way off in Sinai at the time. We all agreed that Cuff would have liked this. I, for one, knew in my heart that he would have liked it very much. I was greatly saddened at his loss, but greatly heartened by the fact that, however briefly, I could say I had known him.

Holmes returned in the afternoon of the fourth day of his disappearance. He merely joined us at meal, walking as in a mesmeric state.

Toward the evening, he became more responsive and slowly we got from him the broad strokes. He too met with Mariam, but his reasons for being there were of a different character altogether from mine. Mariam spoke to him of the Great Library of Alexandria. Despite all our efforts, though, he remained taciturn about the details of his interview.

After another day passed, the priest Tabot reappeared and announced that our visit had ended and that we needed to pack and prepare to leave Sinai. The following morning, he and Ruth escorted us through the valley and back to the cleft by the fountain. As before, the townspeople came out in throngs, this time to see us off. All concerned seemed happy that we were at this juncture. Our hosts seemed grateful to be rid of us, and we were grateful to be returning to our homes.

One thing, though. We had to give our solemn oaths that we would never reveal the location of Sinai—the home of Mariam for all those many centuries. Thus I have made a point of not being too geographically specific in this record.

Each member of the remainder of my expedition—Miss Mitchell, Stanley, Dravot, Carnehan, Huxley, Holmes, and even Hans and the Zulu Bayushtiak—chose this moment to wish the community well and promised to keep their silence.

But it is the words of Miss Mitchell and Bayushtiak that I recall best. Our learned astronomer asked Ruth to convey a message to Mariam. "Please tell your mistress that now I understand that it was she who instilled in me the strength and determination to fight off the Danakil. Please tell her of my gratitude and say that I will keep her with me always."

Bayushtiak spoke in Zulu, which I translated: "My master, The Great One, the Opener of Roads, sent me to protect the white man, Macumazahn, from various and sundry threats, and I believe that I have fulfilled my obligation well. Therefore, I leave this spot with a sense of accomplishment, yet there is much more also. I feel that I have been in the presence of the One who is the maker of the very air that I breathe and the sunlight that warms my face. Never have I felt so much energy as I have felt here, but an energy, indeed a passion, bent on nurturing rather than the fighting for which I was bred. I know full well that it is your mistress who is the font of all these feelings and blessings, and I will remember her in kind as well as I can, evermore."

Once we all had a chance to say our mind, Ruth closed her eyes and responded, mysteriously, as seemed to be the coin of the realm in that far-off hidden spot, with Mariam's voice: "Thank you for your kind prayers, my children. Now go and forge the changes that I have asked in secret ways of each of you. Go in peace, and believe in your uttermost hearts that all my requests will bear fruit: this is not only possible, but inescapable."

And then we were ushered out and we retraced our steps through the narrow cleft to Tabot's chapel. As we prepared to forever leave the chapel, Tabot came to show us what had become of Cuff. He'd been interned in a sheltered corner of the rose garden surrounded by his favorite plants. We were all touched by the respect with which they honored the great detective. After more farewells, and a promise that we would not be troubled again by the Danakil on our return trek, we once again entered that horrible desert.

Thus, this story ends. At that time I didn't know this wouldn't be my only journey to the Red Sea. There was to be another, one that would be forever connected to one of the saddest memories of my life.

We returned to the bay where we found the *Deborah*, the naval vessel that had carried us to Ethiopia, which had been patrolling the coast of the Red Sea while waiting for us. The journey back was uneventful. It took about the same amount of time and effort to get back to the piers as it taken to get to the hidden town called Sinai.

The only aspect of the return journey that proved of interest was that we were finally able to get Holmes to open up somewhat about his experience. According to him, Mariam asked Ruth to take him a naturally cool cavern where he saw numerous tall cases set up and rows and rows of shelves that were crammed with ancient scrolls.

Ruth confirmed that several thousand of the volumes from the Great Alexandrian Library had in fact made their way to her valley some 1,500 years ago and that there was a certain number of their population whose business it was to copy and recopy the scrolls to preserve their content against the passage of time.

Unfortunately, however, Ruth explained that despite his need to study the works, Holmes would have no chance other than the moment at hand. You can imagine his infinite disappointment, as he would have given up everything to stay, or better, to haul away much of what he found there. Ruth made it clear, though, that he and all the rest of our expedition would be leaving in due course. She did ask him if there was anything in particular he would like to see. And he responded immediately by querying about the gospel that seemed to be the source, other than Mark's, of Matthew and Luke. To Holmes's great relief and joy, she showed him the entirety of the memoir written by the magus Gaspar, the very writings that had so excited his hopes and which he had shared with me at the beginning of our journeying.

Whereupon he busied himself copying these pages and others, furiously scribbling, a task that took him all the days he was gone and utterly consumed him.

Here I bid farewell to the Danakil Desert with all its terrible volcanoes and infinite sands. It bears mentioning at this point that the principal reason for our expedition, that of determining the fate of Emperor Theodore II, simply ceased to be a topic of concern or conversation once we were politely ushered into the Chapel of the Immaculate Heart by the priests of the Order of Sainte Mariam the Divine.

The *Deborah* dropped Hans, Bayushtiak, and me at Durban, and then continued on with the rest of our group. I'm sure they all went their separate ways, returning to the lives they were leading before, perhaps richer for the experience, perhaps not. Stanley retired to New York. Professor Mitchell returned to Vassar College with her precious bits of meteorite. However, I am happy to say that it was not long before our paths crossed again, but that is a whole 'nother tale and this is not the time for its telling. Huxley took away his precious bits of bone. The soldiers Danny Dravot and Peachy Carnehan, for all I know, disappeared off the face of the earth. And, of course, Bayushtiak went to report to his master, that horrible dwarf wizard—"the thing that should never have been born"— who, nonetheless, for reasons I can never be sure of, I count among my friends.

Holmes returned to England and his museum, and now and again I hear a rumor or some other tantalizing word that the translation of Gaspar's thoughts from ancient Ethiopian into English was a continuing project. I often wonder about the results of that effort.

—New York *Examiner*, June 22, 20 – –, evening edition, page 26, bottom left corner of paper edition; but nowhere to be found on the *Examiner* website:

AFRICA PARK PROPOSED

Special to the
New York Examiner

UNITED NATIONS, June 22 — Officials of the United Nations today announced that a summit conference has been formed with representatives from the African nations of Eritrea, Ethiopia, Djibouti, Somalia, Kenya, Uganda, Rwanda, The Democratic Republic of the Congo, Burundi, Tanzania, Malawi, Mozambique, Zambia, Zimbabwe, and South Africa to discuss the possibilities and difficulties inherent in merging segments of each of these nations into a single preserve tentatively named The Great Rift Valley Paleoanthropologic Preserve. While the impetus for this giant effort, which is at heart a matter of diplomacy, has not yet been made public, a source, asking for anonymity, suggests that the early spring bombardment of these governments with e-mails and social media, as well as traditional post, with a certain bank safety deposit box number, may have something to do with it. Our source says the box had last been opened in 1885.

THE END

IN THE BEGINNING—
THE JUNIOR WOODCHUCKS' GUIDEBOOK

"Travelers afoot in hot deserts should set their course toward shade!"
—*Junior Woodchucks' Guidebook*

This is a quote from the Dell comic book *Walt Disney's Uncle Scrooge # 7* (1954). That one comic book, which I read when I was nine or ten, has in many ways informed the direction of my imagination for the whole of my life. It is a splendidly written and drawn tale by Carl Barks of Uncle Scrooge McDuck and his nephews, Donald Duck and Huey, Dewey, and Louie, discovering the Seven Cities of Cibola in the American Southwest.

In every possible way, the story you just read is a tribute or homage to *Uncle Scrooge # 7*. Barks' tale and mine both follow a group of people (or ducks) across a hellish desert in the midst of which they discover a lost city. In both cases, the key to the city is a cleft in a cliff (marked by shade in an otherwise featureless wasteland).

While the cover of the Scrooge comic books prominently displayed Walt Disney's name, what I did not know as a child was that Mr. Disney had little to do with Uncle Scrooge. Scrooge was the creation of a man named Carl Barks and the best Scrooge stories—the ones that haunted me were the ones in which the ducks stumbled on a succession of lost lands and cities—Atlantis, the Shangri-La inspired Tralla La, the mountain kingdom of the Incas, the underground land of Terry Fermy, the Labyrinth of the Minotaur, among many others.

It was a full two decades later that I realized that these stories were mainly conceptual pastiches of Sir H. Rider Haggard's tales of lost cities. Barks drew from Haggard (and his offspring, such as, Edgar Rice Burroughs, A. Merritt, and James Hilton) as surely as desert nomads draw water from an oasis well. The magic Barks touched me with—as glorious as it was—was, in a way, recycled magic. Haggard invented the magic, the subgenre of fantasy that has come to be known as the "lost race adventure." (Yes, while I know that other 18th and 19th century authors are sometimes touted as the originators of this type of story, I am unhesitant in bestowing the honor onto Haggard.)

Once I realized this, I began to collect Haggard and found that it was the 18 "memoirs" (12 novels, 2 novellas, and 4 short stories) of Allan Quatermain (especially those featuring his Hottentot aide-de-camp Hans) that resonated with me the most. It was inevitable, then, that I discovered other Quatermain lost memoirs locked inside my own head. The trick was to get them out!

But, with regards to "The Rose of Fire," the above explanation constitutes only half the story of its origins. The other half resulted from my finding several years ago in a dentist's office a copy of *Vanity Fair* magazine (February 1998) that included a cover line: "The Holiest Place on Earth," which referred to the included excerpt from a book about two adventurers seeking Mt. Sinai. This got me to wondering what I would consider the holiest place on Earth, and I decided it had to be the place where the human race came into being—the Great Rift Valley of East Africa, stretching from Ethiopia to South Africa where Australopithecus fossils had been found!

(Curiously, I am not alone in being inspired by *Walt Disney's Uncle Scrooge # 7*. Clearly the opening sequence of *Raiders of the Lost Ark* owes much to it, and I'm gratified that connection has been documented in detail at various web sites, particularly http://www.dialbforblog.com/archives/429.)

🌿 🌿 🌿

THOMAS KENT MILLER—Has authored three H. Rider Haggard/Great Detective pastiche novels—*Sherlock Holmes on the Roof of the World*, *The Great Detective at the Crucible of Life*, and *Allan Quatermain at the Dawn of Time*—which have been published together in the omnibus *Sherlock Holmes In the Fullness of Time* (Rosemill House/www.lulu.com). He is a member of **The Friends of Arthur Machen** and **The Rider Haggard Society**, and has written for *The Weird Tales Collector*, *The Ghosts & Scholars M. R. James Newsletter*, *Faunus: The Journal of the Friends of Arthur Machen*, *Wormwood*, HarperCollins, Borgo Press, Wildside Press, and Hippocampus Press. His other passionate interests are Victorian and Edwardian ghost stories, 19th-century Hudson River School landscape paintings, home theater and multichannel music, and science-fiction movies, the latter of which has resulted in the nonfiction film study *Mars in the Movies: A History* from McFarland Publishers.

CALL OF THE HUNTER

BY ERIK FRANKLIN

The warm African sun beat down through an open window on the cold body of Henry Trasker. He lay face down on the floor of his hotel room, his back towards the open windows. Several members of the local police were holding back the curious onlookers while Detective Ganizani surveyed the scene. He had a few precious minutes to himself before the British consulate, a man who's interfering and busybody antics had caused him endless frustration, appeared on the scene.

Ganizani made a quick appraisal of the room, and could not resist shaking his head. It was typically English, overly ornate and exceedingly elegant. It was as if a wealthy English tourist, which Henry Trasker was, wanted to escape from England for the wilds of African—and not feel he left his home country too far behind when he awoke.

However, it was not the décor that Ganizani was here to investigate. He was a young man, not what one would call handsome, but he carried a determined (if slightly overzealous) authority about him. Ganizani had worked exceedingly hard to please his superiors in the police force, though he approached it in a different manner than the rest. The majority of his fellow officers had become increasingly tough on their own people in an effort to please their English superiors, but Ganizani was careful to be lenient. His very name meant: "to think" and Ganizani was determined to use his brains and become the finest detective in Africa.

His next task was a grim and gruesome one, but it had to be done. The cause of Henry Trasker's death was obvious: an arrow was protruding from the center of his back. To make a thorough examination, Ganizani was forced to, as delicately as he could; remove the arrow from Trasker's back. A slow, but firm tug removed the arrow and Ganizani began to scrutinize it. No blood had seeped out of the open wound once the arrow was dislodged, so the unfortunate man was likely killed during the night. A quick glance at his traditional English evening-wear indicated that the man had not yet changed into his pajamas.

Before Ganizani could make any more progress with the case, he heard a familiar, unwelcome voice yelling at the African officers.

"See here! I am the English consulate, and you can damned well be sure that I am bloody interested when another one of my country men has been murdered!"

"Let him pass..." Ganizani said with a dejected tone in his voice. He had not bothered to disguise his annoyance anymore in the consulate's presence. Seconds later, the consulate walked swiftly into the room, a sour expression on his face. Simon Grint was a man of tall stature, his face reflected a permanent expression of entitlement, as if he were privately disappointed that he was not the king.

"A pleasure to see you again, sir." Ganizani lied.

"A pleasure? I would have thought that my presence is the bane of your existence! After all, every time we see each other it is on account of another murder you have yet to solve... No Englishman is safe on your watch detective! " Simon yelled at him, waving his arms about in a theatrical manner, his wild blue eyes flashing angrily at Ganizani.

To Ganizani's dismay, it was true. This poor man was the sixth in a string of unsolved murders of wealthy Englishmen. Each of them had been found dead in their respective hotel room, all with an arrow in their back. Simon had, of course, been involved in the investigation from the beginning, and had given Ganizani nothing but trouble. The consulate had harassed the African police force with constant demands for updates that they could not provide. Ganizani had personally inspected the rooftops of the area surrounding each of the hotels involved, since it was the most likely place for the archer to position himself. Yet he could find no evidence that the assassin had been there.

"Just think what will happen to Africa!" Simon bellowed at Ganizani "Your people will begin to lose business! After all, what kind of industrialist wants to establish himself in a place where he risks his life just by stepping foot inside your country? And what of tourists? Do you think they would wish to come here and get an arrow in the back? That would be one damned fine souvenir, I must say!"

"Mr. Grint, if you'll please just listen to me for a moment..." Ganizani started, lowering his hands in a pacifying motion. He was, by now, accustomed to Simon's long-winded rants and ravings. It was not that his points were invalid; it was that Simon seemed to be utterly unaware that his tantrums were holding up the investigation.

"I'll tell you, Detective Ganizani, we would never have had this problem if the crimes occurred in England! Scotland Yard would have caught the devil after the first killing! It's all due to the incompetence of the

Africans trying to police themselves! By god, whoever heard of an African detective?"

With the ugly side of Simon beginning to emerge, Ganizani felt he had to head the man off before his tirade spiraled into another international incident. "Mr. Grint, I believe that I have found a solution to our problem..."

"You found the killer then?" Simon said as indignantly and condescendingly as he could manage.

"No, but a happy medium for the both of us. You do not trust the African police, and we wish to show the English that we can handle matters ourselves. We both need a man that we can trust, so I have hired such a man." Ganizani said in a calm, businesslike manner. He had every intention of informing Simon earlier, but the consulate's theatrical performance waylaid the information.

"And what man is this?" Simon replied, crossing his arms, ready to pounce on any name that Ganizani presented.

"My people have given him the name of Macumazahn, which means "Watcher-by-night." His English name should be more familiar to you: Allan Quatermain." Ganizani stated as a matter of pride.

"Quatermain?" Simon said with surprise, his narrow eyebrows raising dramatically on his forehead "That old man? I understand that he is a great hunter and marksman, but what can he possibly know about criminal investigation?"

"That is what I said, but Detective Ganizani was rather persistent," a new voice said, causing both men to look over at the door. Framed by the doorway was a tall man with a whippet-like body who possessed a kindly, but somewhat frail looking bearded face. He was dressed in a modest brown suit, but had a few African trappings about his person. His long, bony fingers played nervously with the brim of the hat he was clutching in his hands. Ganizani smiled as he beheld Allan Quatermain.

"You arrived with perfect timing, Mr. Quatermain. We were just talking about you!"

"Oh dear..." Quatermain said meekly as he looked down "I hope I do not let you fellows down..."

Simon brightened as well. Seeing a fellow Englishman was always a cause for celebration for the consulate. He clapped his arm around Quatermain's shoulders and shook him in a hearty manner. "I know you won't, Mr. Quatermain! A hunter as cunning and persistent as you are will surely catch our killer in no time! Now, here is your crime scene."

"Good lord..." Quatermain said with sadness as he gently knelt down next to the body of Henry Trasker. "The evil that men do to each other... such a wicked waste of life..." Quatermain muttered to himself as he studied the man's position. Ganizani began to tell him the facts of the case, but Quatermain held up a hand when he saw the arrow lying near the body.

"I do not wish to be rude, Detective Ganizani, but is this the arrow that killed him?"

"Yes, I removed it myself," Ganizani confirmed.

"Did you touch the tip?" Quatermain asked him, his eyes wide with alarm. Ganizani shook his head, but his brow furrowed with concern.

"No, I did not."

"Good, be sure not to. For unless I am mistaken, the tip of this arrow is poisoned!" Quatermain said with urgency as he examined the distinctive black markings on the arrow's shaft.

"Poisoned! Why the devil would it be poisoned? Isn't the arrow in the back enough to do a poor fellow in?" Simon said with incredulity.

"The Night's Hand believe there should be no margin for error. Their methods may be barbaric, but the results speak for themselves!" Quatermain insisted. It was an amazing transformation to behold, for many had seen Quatermain as a meek, soft-spoken man in his daily life. However, when his mind was fixed on a point, he became a savage tiger on a midnight hunt. Ganizani laughed, but for a different reason altogether.

"Mr. Quatermain, I do not wish to be rude, but the Night's Hand was a folk story told to my mother when she was but a child! She was told that if one was dishonest and cruel; their enemies would hire the Night's Hand to slay them in the night. It was merely a cautionary tale to ensure that children behaved!"

"Myths and legends all start somewhere... I should know," Quatermain countered, taking a strong dislike to the man's mockery of his theory. "Furthermore, the markings on the arrow match with those associated with the Night's Hand."

"They could be trying to use the myth to build a... a... mystique, is that the right word? Yes, a mystique about themselves." Ganizani said, still unconvinced.

Simon, most curious, walked over to Quatermain and bent down to examine the arrow grasped in his hand. Though he had no idea what he was looking for, he seemed to feel that he could do some good by offering his opinion. Clearing his throat, he interrupted Quatermain's retort to Ganizani.

"I say, Mr. Quatermain, assuming that your theory is correct and the Night's Hand were indeed an actual tribe, could someone be using their weapons of choice to try and implicate them?"

Quatermain walked away from both men and looked out the window. Though he was studying the many rooftops for vantage points, he was also doing his best to see the merits in Simon and Ganizani's point of view. He was unable to shake the feeling that both men were somehow wrong, yet he was unsure as to the correct answer.

"No suspects?" Quatermain inquired.

"They haven't been able to find one!" Simon said, looking down his nose at Ganizani.

Nodding, Quatermain looked back out the window. "I will begin now, and I want you to accompany me, Detective Ganizani. We'll start at the markets."

🌿 🌿 🌿

Entering the hustle and bustle of the nearby open air marketplace, Quatermain thought fondly of the wide, open plains of the African countryside. He could breathe easier standing there, surrounded by the majestic vastness of the plains. He could stretch his limbs. Now, he felt cramped, with the current of the crowd forcing him to move along from stall to stall. Vendors displayed their handmade works of art, fighting for the attention of each foreigner that came into view. Ganizani walked by Quatermain's side, talking over the din of the crowd. He explained the past murders briefly, Quatermain nodding grimly over the gruesome details of each case.

"Of course Simon, that is Mr. Grint, has been a major thorn in my side." Ganizani could not help but vent his frustration to a new ear. "I understand his position, of course. I feel that he complains too much, but does little in the way of being productive. It seems that any chance he gets, he will take the opportunity to insult me, my people, or Africa itself. It is truly difficult to show a man like him respect!"

"I am afraid that you will never get an apology from a man like him, and I hope that you accept mine in its place." Quatermain stated diplomatically, feeling pangs of regret for his fellow countryman's behavior.

"What is it about you, Mr. Quatermain, that makes you different from the others? Your reputation among the Africans has spread far and wide." Ganizani asked, curiosity overcoming him.

Quatermain felt slightly flustered by the question, and his first reaction was to shrug, but he fumbled for an answer. "I am not sure what you mean exactly. I suppose that I do have beliefs that differ from the other Englishmen you may have met. For one thing, I cannot stand English weather, or English cities for that matter. Obviously, I prefer the freedom and warmth of Africa..." he said, hoping that something in his explanation was what Ganizani was looking for.

"But you treat us differently than they do," Ganizani said, and there was the root of his question. Quatermain nodded and gave a more confident answer.

"I feel that people are people, and though I do support my countrymen starting a new life here—it would be hypocrisy to feel otherwise—I do feel that the Africans need to have a say in how they conduct their lives."

"That is more than Simon believes," Ganizani said bitterly. He was about to continue with another rant regardin the much hated English consulate, but something in Quatermain's expression stopped him. The great hunter had his eyes fixed on something, much like a lion stalking its prey. Ganizani tried to follow his gaze, but could not see what had captivated him. Quatermain obliged by indicating whom he had fixed his gaze upon.

"There, do you see her?" he asked the African detective.

Ganizani soon spotted the young woman that Quatermain was watching. She was African, strikingly beautiful with a full figure. Her dark eyes darted from traveler to traveler, as she tried to sell them a wooden flute with black, simplistic tribal markings.

"Yes, she is quite beautiful, Mr. Quatermain. Though, if you do not mind me saying, she seems too young for you." Ganizani said, slightly annoyed that Quatermain had not found something more interesting.

Quatermain still held his gaze, ignoring Ganizani's remark. "Look at her, detective. Do you see the desperation in her eyes? She *needs* to sell that wooden flute."

"Of course she does, it is how she makes her living. Is this relevant to the murders?" Ganizani said, eager to continue along the market path. Quatermain held his place firmly, and though he was a meek man, an air of defiance was clearly written on his face.

"I encourage you to notice two things. First, she is only trying to sell the flute to foreigners. If she was as desperate for money as she looks, she would be trying to sell to Africans as well. Secondly, if you had paid more attention to the "folk stories" related to you as a boy... you would see that the markings belong to the Night's Hand!"

"Mr. Quatermain, while I respect you and your theory, I do sincerely feel that you are wandering down the wrong path. Anyone could have painted those patterns; they are trying to make a simple flute more exotic after all..." Ganizani said in an attempt to rationalize. He felt that he had perhaps put undue strain on Quatermain to get results, and the old hunter was grasping at straws in an attempt to appease and impress him.

"I'll speak with her, but mention nothing of the Night's Hand. I want you stay out of sight. If my suspicions are correct, I want you to follow her until she sells the flute and report back to me." Quatermain said, giving his orders in the same manner that he conducted his famous hunting parties. Taken by his sudden commanding authority, Ganizani nodded and sat on a nearby wooden bench, blending in with the crowd.

Quatermain worked his way through the district and out of the woman's line of sight. When he reentered the crowd, his demeanor was one of a British tourist, acting as if the entire continent of Africa was his personal amusement park. He heard many vendors call out to him, but Quatermain ignored them, and soon enough... he heard her voice.

Turning to her, he saw her alluring face up close. Though he could still sense the desperation in her eyes, she had learned to mask it well. She extended the flute towards him and spoke in an enthusiastic voice.

"Sir, would you like to buy an authentic African flute? It is said to have belonged to a long lost tribe of people, and can be yours for a very reasonable price!" It was a line that she had used over and over, yet she seemed to bring a freshness to it. Quatermain studied the pipe, and no doubt about it, it belonged to the Night's Hand. The dark black and red markings on the wood, painted in a jagged manner, symbolized the prediction of a violent and deadly night.

"A lost tribe you say? How unusual... and what a ghastly pattern that is! Fascinating! Can you tell me about it?" Quatermain pressed, doing his best to seem the ignorant tourist.

"I do not know much about it, I am sorry that I cannot be more helpful. Would you like it? It is only a few of your pounds, sir!" she said quickly. Quatermain noted that she dodged the question about its origin, and another thought occurred to him. He had remembered that the Night's Hand were said to attack only when they heard the call, and he wondered if perhaps this flute could be a key to summoning them.

"I would like to hear the flute before I decide to purchase it. I say, can you perhaps play a little something?"

Her face dropped, and a look of fear momentarily overtook her expression. Though she quickly recovered, Quatermain saw the reaction that he was hoping for. She was somehow connected with the Night's Hand, and knew far more than she was letting on. The woman had returned to her pleasant manner and offered him a charming smile of false naivety.

"I'm afraid that I cannot play a note, sir. However, it is said that this flute brings the player great luck if he attempts a song at midnight," she said, leaning towards him, as if she were sharing a great secret. Quatermain played along, and acted the part of an affronted customer who had become bored with the story.

"I have no idea if this flute works or not, young lady. I shall not purchase an item if I am suspect of its quality. Good day," he said as he walked away from the woman. He heard her call after him, but he kept walking on.

Eventually he found Ganizani and he spoke to the detective with a hurried excitement.

"Listen to me, detective. I believe that the woman selling the flutes has some connection to the murders!"

"More of your Night's Hand theory?" Ganizani said, perturbed.

"I want you to continue following her, and if she sells the flute, report back to me at once. Here is the address I am staying at," Quatermain said, handing him a small piece of paper. Ganizani looked at it unhappily.

"Since when do the police jump at your beck and call?" he inquired.

"I thought that you wanted to solve the murders. If you only brought me in to stave off the consulate's wrath, then shame on you!" Quatermain snapped with uncharacteristic anger, as if a member of his hunting party were carelessly putting others in danger. Sighing, Ganizani met Quatermain's gaze.

"Very well, I'll follow her myself and report back to you later," Ganizani said as he walked away from Quatermain. Quatermain looked after the detective as he disappeared into the crowd, feeling a mixture of anger... and foreboding.

Night had fallen over the city, and Quatermain had begun his vigil, hunting rifle in hand. Looking out at the city, he reminded himself of an earlier conversation that Ganizani and he had just before sunset.

"Mr. Quatermain, the girl has sold the flute!" the detective had said, breathless. Evidently he had sprinted from the scene to Quatermain's location.

"To whom?" was his reply, and he could already feel energy beginning to surge throughout his body, ready to spring into action.

"An Englishman and his wife. I think he was a tourist, because I saw them go back to the Sapphire Hotel after they made the purchase," Ganizani reported, waving his hand in a vague direction towards the hotel.

"I had a feeling she was seeking foreigners. The Sapphire you say? This could prove tricky..." Quatermain said as he began to walk towards the hotel.

"What do you mean?" Ganizani said, dismayed at the prospect of more walking.

The Sapphire Hotel was designed for tourists who were wealthy, but desired a more authentic African experience than the typical luxury hotel. The architecture and décor were kept traditional, yet were crafted specifically for the hotel, giving the establishment the look of a grand safari. When the two reached the hotel, Quatermain confirmed that his fears were well founded and explained them to the tired detective. The Sapphire Hotel offered a beautiful view of the African jungle and countryside, since it was built close to the edge of the city. However, Quatermain pointed out that the hotel was ideal for an assassin who wished to use a bow and arrow, for it was surrounded by a series of large hills that were level with the majority of the rooms.

"It would be a simple, straight shot. A marksman or archer in this case, with a moderate amount of skill, far less than our assassin has demonstrated, could easily pull off the shot." Quatermain explained. "Perhaps fortune favors us, and our English couple is staying in a room facing the town?" Quatermain postulated.

Ganizani regretfully shook his head, "No sir, I had the hotel give me their room number, and it is that one, right there." the detective pointed to a room near the middle of the hotel, naturally facing the hillside.

"Of course it is..." Quatermain said, sighing.

The hills were teeming with thick, healthy vegetation. The tan plains grass that preceded the jungle was tall enough to cover a man up to his thighs, or completely conceal a man lying on his stomach. And this is exactly what Quatermain was doing: lying on his stomach, keeping his hunter's eye on a particular spot... his rifle at the ready. After he had dismissed Ganizani to warn the couple of impending danger, Quatermain had scouted the area to locate the most probable position the shooter would take. When he had settled on the best spot, Quatermain doubled back and looked for the ideal location to be concealed and observe what he theorized to be the assassin's position. Once he had made these choices, Quatermain had hatched a scheme with Ganizani.

"I take it that the couple has been moved to another hotel?" Quatermain asked.

"Yes, they have been moved, though they were most unhappy about it. I said that the police would pay for the room. And I recovered the flute, claiming that the girl had stolen it and it was part of an ongoing investigation." Ganizai said, as if he were reporting to a superior officer. Quatermain smiled, for it was obvious that the young man, if he was this steadfast in his work, would be a fine officer.

"Very well. It is time that we set a trap for our hunter. I would ask you to have the utmost faith in me, for I'm afraid that the plan I have concocted will place you in mortal danger."

After a moment's though, Ganizani looked Quatermain in the eye. "I trust your judgement. I brought you in on the case, after all." Though the detective tried to make light of the matter, there was a severity in his gaze, warning Quatermain not to fail.

"Good point. Now, at midnight, I want you to play the flute, just like the girl told me to," Quatermain instructed.

"But I don't know how to play a flute!" Ganizani protested.

"It's not the song, but the *sound* that is important. Will you do as I say?"

Seeing that he was left with no other options, Ganizani reluctantly agreed.

It was growing late, and the cold night air of Africa was beginning to chill Quatermain to the bone. Still, he was undeterred, having undertaken many adventures in far more severe conditions. Though Quatermain kept his eyes trained on the spot that he had theorized the hunter would shoot his arrow from, he kept looking around, just in case his opponent thought differently than he did. He glanced back at the hotel, and saw that Ganizani had kept the room dark. Perhaps that would delay the assassin as he waited to see any signs of life emanating from the room.

Quatermain was controlling his breathing, making it shallow, rendering him virtually silent whilst steadying his heartbeat. If all went according to his plan, Quatermain would then leap into action at a moment's notice. He lay there with his hunting rifle, for hours on end if need be, ready to fire.

Suddenly, he felt the wind shift around him. It would have been imperceptible to anyone but an experienced adventurer like himself. Someone was coming from the jungle! Quatermain watched closely as the

"I take it that the couple has been moved..."

grass moved ever so slightly against the wind. The hunter found himself impressed by the assassin, and if he had not been looking for the telltale signs of movement, he might have missed him altogether. The assassin was coming closer, though Quatermain could distinguish nothing about him yet.

"In a few moments..." Quatermain thought to himself, "I will see if this assassin is an experienced man, who conceals himself like a ghost—or if he is an arrogant man, whose success has weakened a sense of caution."

As Quatermain put the rifle's scope to his eye, he saw that the latter was true. Standing up in the middle of the field, the assassin had made the critical mistake of letting the moon be at his back, thus causing him to stand out against the night. True, the assassin would have had no way of knowing that Quatermain would be lying in ambush, but "one can never be too careful" as Quatermain often said.

Quatermain could see that the man was athletically built, and clearly was used to running, fighting, and hunting. Though he had made a foolish mistake by standing, the assassin at least knew as much as Quatermain about positioning himself for the ideal shot. Backlit by the moon, it was impossible to make out any details about the hunter, but Quatermain saw that his archer's stance was perfection itself.

Quatermain had been waiting for the sound of the flute to begin playing, thinking that on a quiet night like this, he could have heard it, even faintly. However, there was no sound, yet the assassin was ready to fire his arrow. Quatermain was forced to act!

Raising his rifle, Quatermain aimed at the assassin. It took Quatermain milliseconds to decide where to shoot. If he hit the assassin's bow and arrow, which had been his first impulse, he would destroy evidence useful to the African police and English authorities. Killing the assassin would also yield no information. Shooting him in the arm would prevent him from firing his bow, but would still allow him to escape... and he would still be a threat. The only logical choice, as far as Quatermain could see, was to shoot the assassin in the upper thigh. It would be painful, if not near impossible, for the assassin to run, and the sudden impact of the bullet would cause his arrow to miss its target.

Having been a marksman for a great many years, Allan Quatermain was the finest shot in all of Africa (some suspected that he was the greatest marksman on earth). His eyes adjusted perfectly to the dark, like a jungle cat. Quatermain raised his rifle and fired! The loud crack filled the air, and then a deep, wounded cry came from the assassin. His body had jerked with the impact, causing the arrow to go wild and land harmlessly into the tall grass. Despite his wound, the assassin attempted to flee, and Quatermain bounded after him!

The man looked to be much younger and stronger than Quatermain, so the old hunter hoped that the injury would help to even the odds. The assassin, despite his slower pace, was fleeing in the direction of the jungle when Quatermain caught up with him. He loudly cocked his rifle, a sharp, distinctive sound that was meant as a warning. The assassin stopped in his tracks, knowing that taking another step would mean a bullet in his back.

Quatermain kept his rifle level, slowly advancing, as the assassin turned to face him. Revealed in the moonlight, the assassin's makeup was now visible. He was African, and his body was covered in the cryptic, distinctive midnight-blue markings of the Night's Hand. He glared at Quatermain, angered and resentful at the man who crippled him.

Clearing his throat, Quatermain spoke firmly to the man, "You can't run, so you'd better answer my questions. I know that you work for the Night's Hand... but why are the Night's Hand killing again? Who is behind this?"

"Whenever a man... with a heart of evil... needs his enemies to die... he performs the ritual... and the Night's Hand will be his instrument..." the assassin answered. His English was surprisingly clear and distinct, and Quatermain guessed that he had lived among Englishmen in order to pick up the subtle nuances of the language. Quatermain had also recognized the phrase from a grim chant among the African people. The assassin was merely repeating common folklore passed down through the generations.

"As a matter of curiosity, who taught you how to shoot so well?" Quatermain asked, genuinely interested.

"You know too much, Mr. Quatermain!" the assassin yelled! The darkness had concealed the man's movements, and Quatermain did not see the flash of a dagger thrown at him until it was too late! He did not have time to dodge, so he moved his rifle across his chest to deflect the flying blade. The dagger struck his rifle, and the force knocked him off balance. The assassin was on him like a flash!

Tackling Quatermain, the assassin was positioned on top of the hunter and he closed his hands around the old man's throat! Quatermain could feel intense pressure choking him as the assassin squeezed the breath out of him. The assassin's face twisted in rage. Quatermain reached for his gun, but it had been knocked away when they toppled over each other. Despite the assassin's great strength, Quatermain did have one advantage over the man: his reach. Quatermain stretched his arms up and with his left hand, forced the man's chin backwards. Quatermain began to feel his consciousness slipping away, and he was gasping for air, but the assassin showed no sign of weakness. Through blurred vision, Quatermain could see that the man's neck was exposed now; his left hand had managed to push the assassin's head back quite far.

Everything was beginning to grow dark, and with an act of desperation, Quatermain threw all of his remaining strength into his next move. The old hunter had balled up his right fist and slammed it directly into the assassin's throat with all of his might! The assassin's whole body shuddered as his hands flew up to his throat protectively. It was his turn to start gasping for air. Struggling to get free, Quatermain had enough strength to seize his rifle by the gun barrel. He swung the weapon around, felt the momentum stop and he heard a loud crack as the butt of the rifle struck the side of the assassin's head. Quatermain was still struggling to regain his senses as he got back on his feet, his rifle ready.

He saw that the assassin was lying flat on the ground, though he was still breathing. Quatermain felt relieved, for he needed the man alive for information. As the soreness and constriction around his throat lessened, Quatermain breathed in heavily. He saw Ganizani running towards him, and a look of shock came over his face as he saw the body of the assassin lying sprawled on the grass before Quatermain.

"Is he...?" Ganizani started to ask, noticing the bloody wound on the assassin's head.

"No, but he'll wake up with an awful headache." Quatermain said as he straightened up, his muscles sore from the struggle, though his breathing was gradually returning to normal.

"I came running as soon as I heard the shot, I am sorry that I was not here sooner." Ganizani said as he examined Quatermain.

"Detective... did you play the flute at midnight, because I could not hear a thing." Quatermain asked curiously.

"Yes, yes I did. The strange thing was that I could not hear anything either! At first I thought I might have been doing something wrong, but that seemed unlikely." Ganizani admitted.

"Well, I know we will have plenty of questions for our assassin here, but they'll have to wait until morning when this fellow wakes up." Quatermain said as he helped Ganizai carry the body to the police station.

Quatermain trudged through the town early that morning, his body still aching and tired from the night before. He had been summoned by the British consulate to meet at sunrise, requesting a private conversation with just him, and Quatermain was irritated that Ganizani was being excluded. He did not care to be ordered about like a dog, it greatly annoyed him. Quatermain reminded himself that he was technically in the employment of the English government and he supposed that meant he must do what they said.

He arrived at the consulate's office and was met outside by Simon's secretary. He was a stout, and serious faced man with a neatly trimmed military mustache. His demeanor was one of professionalism, and his desk reflected absolute order and efficiency.

"Hello, sir, my name is Corporal Anthony Stewart, and how may I be of service to you?"

"Hello Corporal, my name is Allan Quatermain, and I have an appointment to see Mr. Simon Grint." Quatermain said, taking his hat off as a sign of respect.

"*The* Allan Quatermain! It is an honor, sir! Mr. Grint should be arriving shortly, so I will ask you to wait inside, if that is agreeable?" Anthony opened the doors and motioned him in. Quatermain could not help but feel embarrassed... he longed, once again, for the quiet, humble life that always seemed to elude him.

Anthony closed the door behind Quatermain. Looking around Simon's office, Quatermain saw the typical trappings of an English official: a British flag on the wall, a tea set, various official papers and volumes. However, he became interested that the consulate had a fair number of books and documents about Africa and its cultures. Walking over to the small bookshelf, he noticed that several pages were earmarked. Quatermain took note, and thought it odd that Ganizani would berate a man who, while imperfect, seemed to be taking great pains to understand a culture that he was assigned to cooperate with.

The door opened and Quatermain looked across to see the long, frowning face of Simon Grint as he entered the office. He managed a practiced smile upon seeing Quatermain.

"Allan Quatermain, good to see you my boy! Good to see you indeed! I say, frightfully sorry to be late. An unfortunate incident occurred that I had to take care of immediately. Please accept my apology." Simon said as he shook Quatermain's hand. The consulate sat behind his desk with a sigh, and motioned Quatermain to the leather chair opposite the desk.

"What has happened?" Quatermain asked.

"I need to hear what happened last night first." Simon replied after a moment's pause.

"I thought that Detective Ganizani would have reported everything to you already," Quatermain said, feeling confused.

"Yes, he did, and he was thorough as per usual. However, I would like to hear the story from you. After all, you saw the assassin firsthand and single-handedly apprehended him."

Quatermain squirmed in his seat, feeling uncomfortable. He did not like to be the center of attention, and even if one were to convince him to retell one of his past adventures, Quatermain would downplay his part to such a degree that he might have been likened to a ghost observing the scenes unfold. Such was the case with this story, as he told it to Simon with his accustomed humility. Simon listened with great interest, nodding sternly at appropriate points. Quatermain wrapped up his tale, but started to feel an unease in the atmosphere.

"Since I have now related what happened... perhaps it is your turn to tell me your news." Quatermain said, while trying to anticipate what Simon's ominous tidings may be.

"So that is all the assassin said... that cryptic thing about a man with an evil heart..." Simon said as he stood up again, looking out his window at the village people wandering about below in the street.

"That, and he threatened me, as I have told you."

"Yes... yes... well I wish that he would have said something a bit more useful to you..." Simon mused regretfully "we found the assassin dead this morning."

"What?" Quatermain said, feeling the blood drain from his face. "I know that I got a bit rough with the man, but I did not think I hit with enough strength to..."

"No, no, you can relax Allan," Simon said as he patted Quatermain on the shoulder "he did not die from his wounds. The police concluded that he had concealed a small vial of poison in the heel of his sandal, the same type of venom he used on his victims. A fitting end for him really, all things considered."

"Hopefully this will stop the murders, but I'm afraid there are several loose ends that need to be tied up." Quatermain said as he regained his composure.

"I agree, but what do you think the loose ends are?"

"To begin with, the matter of the silent flute. And the girl selling them.

I may have spoken too soon, for the Night's Hand are many, according to the old tales. There may be other assassins, and she could be the key to finding them!" Quatermain said, eager to find her trail once again. He was growing impatient with this conversation; every moment he spoke with Simon delayed him finding the girl. To his chagrin, Simon had a worried expression on his face, and Quatermain knew that the consulate was not finished with him yet.

"Very good Allan, but I am afraid that there is a somewhat... unpleasant... angle that we need to investigate." Simon said delicately, yet with an air of authority.

"What?"

"Why did the police not properly search the assassin? Why have you been more successful in apprehending the assassin, in a day no less? The police have been working on this for weeks without a single lead?" Simon spoke bluntly, and Quatermain found himself at a loss. "I do not trust Detective Ganizani."

"He seems to be trustworthy to me," Quatermain said, feeling the need to defend the detective. Simon remained unmoved.

"Though he follows protocol well enough and toes the line, he is not loyal to the crown, and believe me, he has no fondness for England. His family has been involved with anti-English activities, you know. Rumor has it that he used his influence with the police to keep his father out of jail during a skirmish with some English officers." Simon stated with a bitterness in his voice.

"And you feel that he has been trying to sabotage the situation?" Quatermain said, hoping to gain further insight into Simon's frame of mind.

"Alas, what I feel and what can be proved are two entirely different things. I'm going to ask that this conversation remain between us, Mr. Quatermain, for the time being. In the meantime, I am going to ask you to keep working with Ganizani... but keep your guard up and your eyes open."

Quatermain looked Simon square in the eyes... "I always do."

The two parted with a handshake. As Quatermain left the office, he felt the same strange feeling of uneasiness wash over him. Though he was beginning to count on Ganizani as a friend, he reexamined the events that had taken place between them. He had been correct about the Night's Hand being involved, yet Ganizani did his best to dissuade him from this train of thought... and if Quatermain had followed his advice, the location would have led nowhere. Furthermore, it seemed that Ganizani resisted or was reluctant to participate in many of Quatermain's plans. It could be his personality, unwilling to attempt any notion that was not his invention, or was it something else? Ganizani had personally sent for him to be involved in the case, so perhaps Simon's suspicions were based on paranoia, or they simply did not like each other and were venting their frustrations to him.

Quatermain headed towards the police station, and saw Ganizani waiting for him outside, nervously bending the edges of a straw hat in his hand. Quatermain walked up to him, and Ganizani sighed in shame.

"I am sorry Mr. Quatermain, but we did all we could. The assassin died in his cell. It was..."

"Simon told me all about it. What happened?"

"As yet, we are not sure. Somehow he managed to poison himself. This is truly a disgrace... a black mark on my career."

Deciding to test the detective, Quatermain feigned ignorance. "How did the poison get past your men?"

"We do not know. We had performed a complete search of the assassin and found nothing."

"I see. What about his sandals? The Night's Hand were known to keep a last vial of poison in their heels." Quatermain fibbed. In truth, he had never heard of the assassins performing such a feat, and he wondered how Ganizani would react.

"Mr. Quatermain, the man came to us barefoot." Ganizai said with great confusion.

Quatermain could not tell if the detective was lying or not. All he knew was that either Ganizani was hiding something... or Simon was lying to him.

"I will be staying in town, since there is nothing for me to do here. You know where to find me." Quatermain said, disguising his reaction to Ganizani's comment. The two parted ways, but as soon as Ganizani was out of sight, the hunter went in a different direction. He moved along the outside walls of the police station until he spotted, at a vacant corner of the building, a large, stinking pile of garbage yet to be collected.

Sifting through the trash as stealthily as he could, Quatermain spotted exactly what he was afraid of: a pair of sandals... and one had a slit in the heel. Quickly placing the sandals back where he found them, Quatermain could not help but feel that something more was amiss than the initial conspiracy that presented itself. It certainly appeared that Ganizani was lying, but Quatermain took the detective to be a man of obvious intelligence.

The great hunter thought it unlikely that a man such as Ganizani would so clumsily attempt to dispose of evidence.

Quatermain wandered through town, trying to decide how he felt about Simon and Ganizani. Their mutual dislike and distrust of each other made finding the truth even more taxing. He doubted that the Night's Hand, if they still existed, would stop the assassination of foreigners just because one of their order had fallen. The only lead he had was the mysterious, exotic woman in the marketplace. Quatermain would have to find her and follow her without being detected.

Navigating through the city, Quatermain was finding that he preferred to be stalking among the brush as opposed to buildings. He thought it unlikely that she would be in the same place twice, the Night's Hand would have probably moved her, lest she begin to attract unnecessary suspicion.

Eventually, he found her outside of the hotel district of the city. Pressing himself up against the corner of a building, Quatermain watched as she attempted to solicit the various foreigners she saw into buying the flutes. He still wondered about the significance of the flutes, but figured that would be answered in time. The sun was beginning to set and she was on the move, and that meant that he would be close behind.

Quatermain found himself out in the wilds once more, and he was cursing his circumstances. He was unprepared for the hunt, with only a small pistol and knife for defense. He thought that following the girl would give him answers, so he had dispensed with any preparations that would have normally been deemed necessary.

The young woman kept on walking through the brush, heading in a straight line seemingly towards a swamp. She would glance behind her shoulder, as if she was suspicious of possibly being followed. As an experienced hunter, Quatermain was able to keep a close eye on her body and predict each of her movements. Whenever she started to turn, he was able to duck and avoid being spotted.

It had occurred to Quatermain, however, that the young woman may have had some indication that he was on her heels, and was deliberately leading him into a trap. It was a risk that he would have to take, though he was unsure if he would be able to improvise an escape.

Suddenly the woman stopped. She did not turn around this time, but instead reached into her waistband and removed the flute she was trying to sell. Taking a deep breath and placing it to her lips, she began to play the flute, though Quatermain could hear no sounds.

A sharp pain suddenly struck Quatermain in the side of the neck! The woman had somehow signaled to an unseen accomplice to shoot him! He wrenched the small dart from his neck as the world began to swim around him. Quatermain examined the dart quickly, and he recognized the familiar aroma of a sedative used by some tribes to immobilize their prey. He saw the young woman turn around to face him, a dark, frighteningly pleasant smile crossing her face.

The darkness enveloped Quatermain as he felt himself collapse to the earth.

When Quatermain awoke, he found himself in a wooden cage. It had been fashioned from the branches of a strong tree, and tied together with thick rope. Quatermain was weak, and breaking out would have been an impossibility. He was also aware of a swinging sensation, and when he looked down, he saw that he was suspended over a dark, murky green swamp. A sinking feeling came over him as he watched the back of an enormous crocodile glisten against the moonlight as it glided effortlessly across the surface. Looking around, Quatermain saw that there were sheer rock walls surrounding the swamp, and a small waterfall was providing the ambience.

Across the way, Quatermain watched as the young woman observed him. She was standing on one of the few rocks that was jutting out. A rope ladder was hanging over her. It was the only means of access to the ledge.

"Who... who are you?" Quatermain said in a faltering tone, the drug still taking its toll, dulling his senses.

"Adisa—" the woman said in a silky voice. It flowed beautifully off of her tongue, which made her seem all the more sinister. "—and you are in the palm of the Night's Hand."

As his vision cleared, Quatermain saw that the sheer rock faces were decorated with various African symbols and paintings. They greatly resembled the works that depicted the Night's Hand, and Quatermain surmised that he was in their lair. No doubt the cage he was in was meant to torture prisoners.

"But why... why me?" Quatermain asked. "Why are you sparing me?"

"We still have use for you, Mr. Quatermain—" Adisa said "—you will

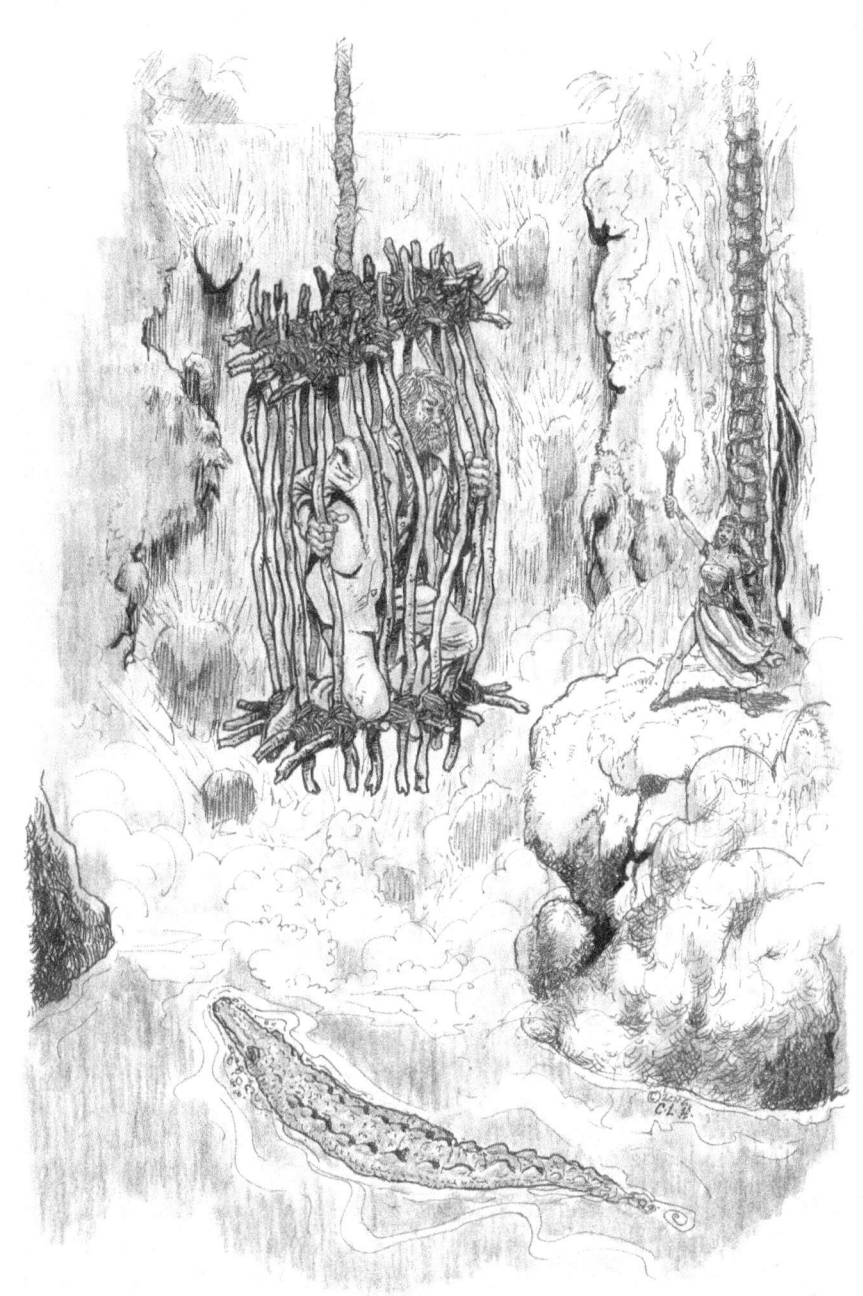

"…you are in the palm of the Night's Hand."

persuade the English to stop their invasion of Africa and the pillaging of its people."

"But I've always felt that the Africans should have a say in their affairs... why single me out for this... this task?" Quatermain said, fighting through to clear the fog in his mind.

"We have killed scores of you English to send a message... but your people's arrogance persists. Many more will die if you do not convince them to leave. You, the great Allan Quatermain, are respected among your people as an... I think the term is... great white hunter? If they will not respect the will of the Night's Hand, then they will listen you!"

"You... you want me to do *what* exactly?" Quatermain asked, unsure of what task he was supposed to undertake. He was also failing to understand the motivations of the Night's Hand. They had historically been a sheltered, insulated group of assassin mercenaries. Why they would suddenly take a political interest in Africa was perplexing to him. However, he was more focused on his immediate fate.

Adisa waved her hand forward, and another member of the Night's Hand, adorned in the same body paint that Quatermain had seen on the first assassin that he encountered, walked around the waterfall with a bow and arrow in hand. Quatermain noticed that the man was barefoot, and clung to the slippery rock face with a certain hesitation showing in his muscles. This assassin could not have been a member of the group for long, Quatermain decided. The second assassin placed a piece of paper on the end of his bow tip and shot it at Quatermain's cage. The message imbedded itself into one of the corner posts. Quatermain removed it and unfolded the paper.

"It's blank!" he exclaimed with confusion. Adisa nodded.

"That is because you will write the message, Quatermain. Write it in your own blood! You will tell the English to leave, and we will deliver your message to the authorities."

"I doubt that the word of one man can turn back an empire..." Quatermain attempted to reason, but Adisa would have none of it.

"Not after they see your body..." she threatened.

"If you are going to kill me, what incentive do I have to write this note?" Quatermain said, crossing his arms. The poison had worn off and he had fully come to his senses. Though he could see no way out of his predicament now, he was beginning to form several ideas on how to escape. However, judging by Adisa's face, she had carefully thought of a counter to his possible protests.

She waved for another assassin, and moments later two bodies emerged from around the waterfall. A large, muscular assassin held Ganizani in a choke hold, a knife to his throat! The detective appeared weak, with evident bruising on his face. Quatermain was surprised by his appearance, but a thought crept into his mind: it could be a trap! If Ganizani was behind the murders, then this could be part of an elaborate deception.

"Write the letter, or I cut his throat and feed him to the crocodile!" Adisa demanded, a fierceness emerging from her dark eyes.

Quatermain looked into Ganizani's eyes, and saw a pleading expression. Though Ganizani may be involved, Quatermain realized that he could not bear an even more terrible thought: what if the detective was innocent and if Quatermain refused to write the letter, he would be killing an innocent man!

"Very well..." Quatermain acquiesced, as he pricked his finger on a splinter of the wooden cage. He felt the pain shoot through his finger. Quatermain put the bloody tip to the end of the page and begin to scrawl a message. Though he concentrated on his writing, he looked up to see Adisa watching his every movement. A half glance over at Ganizani confirmed that he was in agony, and Quatermain began to trust the detective again.

"If he resists... kill him. We will improvise."

Adisa spoke to the two assassins in her native tongue, but Quatermain could understand. She gave them orders to keep watching the two men while she went back to the "meeting place" to report on their progress. "To whom is she reporting?" Quatermain wondered as he worked on the letter. She seemed frightened in the marketplace, and he wondered how she could act so cool and confident here. Adisa was clearly afraid of failing her superior, and Quatermain wondered how this could be exploited later. In truth, his letter was of no use to anyone; he had not bothered to make a coherent sentence, but was stalling for time instead.

Quatermain, while pretending to write, was observing the crocodile at the bottom of the swamp. It had grown to a massive size, perhaps twenty feet long, but it also seemed to have grown too large for the swamp. With the steep rock faces, Quatermain estimated that the only food source it was allowed to have were the poor, unfortunate souls that the Night's Hand needed to have disappear. It must have been starving...

Quatermain let his arm, the one with the bleeding finger, drop down so that it was dangling below the cage. He feigned weakness, as if the drug was overcoming him once more. He immediately heard the assassins protest and order him to keep writing, but he watched as the blood from his finger fell onto the swamp water. It spread out gently, and the crocodile's interest peaked. Quatermain looked above him, and saw that the cage was suspended by a thick rope hanging from a sturdy tree branch. He was unsure of how everything would unfold, but this was the only chance he had.

By now, the crocodile had swam around swiftly and positioned itself underneath the cage, its neck craned upwards and its eerie, luminescent eyes fixed on Quatermain's arm. The assassins and even Ganizani were frantically yelling at Quatermain to pull his arm up. The crocodile leapt out of the water, its massive jaws opened to a frightening expanse! Quatermain then yanked his arm out of reach and quickly shifted his body to the side. The cage rattled and shook from the force of the crocodile's bite! The creature had sunk its teeth into the corner of the cage, and disappointed that it did not taste the meat that it desired, it thrashed its head about, breaking open the cage door and collapsing one of the side walls.

The force of the crocodile's attack also caused the cage to swing freely from the tree branch. Quatermain held onto the back wall of the cage as he felt himself hurdle forwards and backwards, waiting for the right time to jump to the ledge. Ganizani seized this opportunity to free himself. Since the assassin holding him was concentrating on the scene of Quatermain's struggle, he did not feel when Ganizani grabbed his knife arm. Ganizani then fiercely shoved the assassin's body against the wall, and the two began to grapple.

The crocodile had splashed violently as it crashed into the swamp once again, and it was enraged. It watched as Quatermain leapt from the swinging cage and grabbed for the cliff face. Quatermain fell short of the cliff, and his hands clutched against the slippery rock. As Quatermain struggled to get a foothold, he found himself ambushed from two directions. Below him, the angry crocodile was not about to be denied his meal, and it swam towards Quatermain. Above Quatermain, the assassin stood, following Adisa's order to kill him if he attempted to escape. He pulled his bow back, getting ready to plunge an arrow into Quatermain. The crocodile was getting closer, and Quatermain felt his grip slipping even further...

Then the great hunter summoned the strength to raise himself up, and reached his arm out. He caught the assassin by the ankle and pulled him off his feet. The assassin somersaulted over Quatermain and fell into the swamp with a terrified yell. The crocodile, an opportunist and scavenger by nature, lunged towards him! With the beast distracted and dealing with the assassin, Quatermain forced the rest of his body onto the ledge and looked over to see how Ganizani was faring.

The detective had managed to gain the upper hand in the conflict, and threw a solid right cross punch into the assassin's face. Ganizani watched as the assassin dropped to the ground, unconscious. Quatermain and Ganizani's eyes met and they nodded to each other. They both knew they would endure, and Ganizani was impressed by Quatermain's feat. He had underestimated the older man, but would feel foolish to admit it. Improvising a rope with some low hanging vines, Ganizani hog-tied the defeated assassin and then made his way over to Quatermain, who gave the rope ladder a tug to test its strength.

Below them, the crocodile's struggle with the assassin had ended, and the two survivors did their best not to look at the grisly scene below them.

"He should be out for some time." Ganizani said, pointing to the assassin on the ground. "When I get back to the station, I'll send some men to bring that one back for interrogation, and this time, he will be in the cell naked!" Ganizani assured Quatermain.

"No, there is something else at work here. We need to act fast." Quatermain spoke between breathes. He grabbed onto the rope ladder and began to climb out of the pit "We need to find that woman, Adisa, and hopefully she will lead us to her superior!"

❀ ❀ ❀

Though Adisa had a head start on Quatermain and Ganizani, the two were able to track her. The moon provided the only light, but Ganizani observed that the darkness did not seem to hinder the old adventurer in the least. Quatermain studied the soil and the brush where Adisa had walked, and saw that she was taking another deliberate path, though this one was winding and would be confusing to the untrained eye. Quatermain knew from experience that this time, Adisa was deliberately attempting to cover her tracks. Therefore, Quatermain hoped, she would lead him to the last pieces of the puzzle in this sinister and deadly affair.

Ganizani talked while Quatermain tracked, "You see, it was not that I did not trust you Mr. Quatermain, but I was afraid for your life, so I decided to follow you."

"I see. I appreciate the thought." Quatermain replied, only half listening.

"However, I also wanted to find you to inform you of a discovery that I have made. The victims have a connection beyond being English."

Quatermain's ears perked up as he looked to Ganizani "Yes? What is the connection?"

"Simon had told us that the people who were being murdered were tourists, but this is only a half truth. They were on tour, yes, but all of them had industrial connections abroad, and, according to their associates in the British Isles, all of them were in Africa on business!" Ganizani spoke rapidly, his enthusiasm getting the better of him. "So you see, the Night's Hand's motivations are clear as crystal! They want to frighten the foreigners away from Africa!"

"I hate to disagree with you, but I feel that you are only half correct." Quatermain said, hoping that he would not deflate the detective's pride too much with his next statement. "You see, I think that what you suggest *is* the motivation for the murders, but it is not the Night's Hand that is behind it."

"Then who could it be?" Ganizani said, at a loss.

"Simon Grint." Quatermain said, much to the surprise of Ganizani. The detective stopped in his tracks momentarily, as he processed the information. After a few moments, he spoke quietly to Quatermain.

"Why do you suspect him? I admit that I dislike the man greatly, but... what evidence do you have? And what about his motive for the murders? He has nothing to gain as far as I can see."

"I admit that I have no evidence thus far, which is why you will be invaluable. I need you to confirm what I hope to see. Then, if my hunch is correct, all of the murders will be solved in one fell swoop."

"What do you hope to see?"

"A meeting between Adisa and Simon. I admit that I am, once again, stepping into danger ill-prepared, but we may not be able to catch them together again."

"But the security at the consulate is very strict. I am not sure that we would be able to watch them unobserved." Ganizani reasoned.

Quatermain, still looking at Adisa's footsteps, waved away Ganizani's protest. He was fixated on the hunt, and finding Adisa on the path was his only focus.

"They would not meet at his office because Simon would not want to be implicated. They are meeting..." Quatermain trailed off, raising his head to see the path in front of him. He spotted several small, flickering orange lights in the distance. He reasoned that they were torches, and every instinct told him that he would find Adisa and Simon "...they are meeting there! We have to hurry!"

"I will admit, Mr. Quatermain, that I do not leave the city often. I confess that I have no idea what lies beyond this point." Ganizani confessed, wishing that he could have been more help in the situation.

"I know this area," Quatermain said "and there is a shortcut. I think I know where she is going... but I wish I had a bloody rifle!" he snapped, allowing a rare bit of frustration to escape his lips.

Taking Quatermain's shortcut, the two made their way to the edge of a hill, where they were able to survey the situation more clearly. Lying prone, Quatermain and Ganizani hid among the brush grass as they watched Adisa emerge from a nearby jungle clearing. She made her way towards a long, rickety, rope and wood bridge, and then waited patiently. A river was raging beneath the bridge, and it was an eighty foot fall should one lose their footing.

The torches were glowing orange on the other side of the bridge. This is where Quatermain suspected that Simon was lurking, and the fires were a signal for Adisa to show that he was waiting for her. Soon enough, Quatermain watched as a male figure strolled across the bridge, adjusting his clothing. Quatermain reasoned it to be Simon, and he saw that Adisa grew visibly tense at the sight of him.

"What should we do?" Ganizani whispered.

"Watch and wait... we act only if it is necessary." Quatermain insisted. In truth, he was itching to get to the bottom of the whole affair, but knew the virtue of patience and letting an enemy hang himself.

"Where is my brother!" Adisa demanded before Simon could say anything. The consulate gave a condescending laugh as he crossed the bridge.

"Do you have Quatermain's letter?" he countered, deliberately avoiding her question. As he came into the light, Quatermain could see that he was no longer in his formal consulate dress, but wearing a safari outfit, more befitting an explorer. The less constricting outfit revealed a rather fit looking physique, suggesting that Simon was not exactly the confined office worker that he pretended to be.

"He is writing it now! Once he is finished my men will kill him and that foolish detective, as you have ordered. Now where is my brother!" she said, not attempting to hide the urgency in her voice.

"He is alive, rest assured, but I still need the Night's Hand to finish a few more important tasks for me." Simon said as he stepped off the bridge to speak with Adisa face to face.

"You said that once we dealt with Quatermain you would let him go!

The Night's Hand are a tribe founded on honor and—"

"*Honor*! You are a group of assassins! There is no honor in that! Your need to be feared and respected by your fellow Africans is not honor. As they say... 'pride goeth before the fall.'" Simon laughed with an incredulous expression on his face.

"*You* cannot claim to be a man with honor! You order your fellow countrymen murdered so you can have a larger hold of interest in African business! You have taken my brother as hostage! You have left me no choice but to do your bidding!" Adisa shot back.

"Merely an insurance policy... I am a businessman after all and I do not claim to be honorable... but you must face facts, my dear Adisa... when I was exploring this continent and came across your tribe, you were all but forgotten! Your proud sect of assassins had dwindled to a pitiful few amateurs remaining! The Night's Hand was nothing but a fairy tale to the African people! I gave you a new life and purpose! I alone have resurrected the Night's Hand, and when Quatermain finishes his letter..."

"You exploited us! You took advantage of our situation! I made a horrible mistake when I agreed to your terms!" Adisa shouted.

"May I remind you what will happen if you try to break our agreement?" he said with a smug expression on his face. In the blink of an eye, she had pulled a dagger from her waistband and grabbed Simon by the collar. Holding the knife against his throat, she was ready to make the fatal move, but Simon still held his composure. "Kill me and your brother dies." Simon grinned. The knife was still at his throat, but Adisa reluctantly stayed her hand. "It pains me to admit, but I do need the effect the Night's Hand delivers to frighten my countrymen out of Africa. However, I am beginning to have my doubts about your use..."

"I am the leader of the Night's Hand! I alone know the secret of..."

"The silent flutes? Oh dear girl, your brother told me about that after his third day of torture. I know that your tribe are the only ones trained to hear its unusual harmonics... when the poor fool you sold the flute to decides to play it, your assassins hone in on the noise and strike. Clever and totally untraceable, and the murder appears to be without motive."

"Then... then you... know how we work..." she said, beginning to realize the larger implications of his statement.

"So you see, as a businessman, I find you to be nothing more than a middleman. I can easily convince the assassins of the Night's Hand to follow me... without holding their families hostage. Pride, you know. In any case, you have become unnecessary!"

With a burst of speed, Simon knocked the knife from her hand and kicked Adisa firmly in the stomach. She doubled over in pain, and Ganizani instinctively leapt from the brush towards Simon! Quatermain tried to stop him, but the detective was too quick. Simon was surprised as Ganizani tackled him to the ground, where the two began to wrestle each other, kicking up a small cyclone of dirt and foliage.

"Anthony!" Simon yelled in the struggle.

Quatermain had held his ground and was getting ready to assist Ganizani when a glimmer in the forest caught his eye. He held back and saw a rifle emerge from a nearby bush, sparkling in the moonlight. Quatermain recognized the man who was aiming the rifle... it was Simon's secretary, Anthony! Quatermain watched as Anthony tracked the struggling pair with his rifle, but he was having difficulty getting a bead on Ganizani.

Quatermain raced down the hill, making more noise than he would have liked. Anthony wheeled around, firing a shot at Quatermain in his panic. The bullet harmlessly sailed past Quatermain, imbedding itself in a tree close by. Anthony knew it was futile to attempt to reload the rifle, Quatermain was rushing at him and would have been upon him had he tried. So he flipped the rifle in his hands and swung the butt of it at Quatermain's skull. Ducking the wild swing, Quatermain grabbed the rifle and began to struggle with Anthony.

Ganizani, though a strong man, was losing his battle. Simon fought with precision and efficiency. No movement was wasted as he continued to pummel the detective. Adisa had recovered from Simon's blow, and looked desperately for her knife that was kicked around in the struggle. After locating it, she looked to Simon, but he met her gaze. It was probable that he could anticipate and dodge Adisa's knife throw, so she looked to Anthony and Quatermain instead. Anthony was overpowering Quatermain, but his back was to her. Though she knew that saving Quatermain would mean ruin for her and the Night's Hand, Adisa had had enough. Quatermain, she understood, was a man who loved and respected Africa, and Simon was a man who sought to exploit it. She threw the knife with deadly accuracy...

Quatermain watched as a pained expression crossed Anthony's face, his teeth clenched and his eyes squinted. His grip on the rifle tightened and then relaxed as Anthony's hands slowly let go of the barrel. His body dropped to the ground, dead. Quatermain took the rifle in his hands and stripped a few bullets off of Anthony's belt. While loading the gun, he looked up to see Simon standing over Ganizani, the former being the clear winner of the fight. The detective lay on the ground motionless, but still breathing. Turning away from Ganizani, Simon drew a pistol from inside his vest and aimed the weapon at Adisa's heart.

"Mr. Quatermain..." Simon said as he caught his breath, though his gun arm was remarkably still. "I know you are one of the finest hunters in the world... I am not so bad myself..." he said with a smile Quatermain found disconcerting.

"Put the gun down, Simon... it is over!" Quatermain ordered, his rifle pointed at Simon's chest. He doubted that Simon would follow his request, and Quatermain knew that Simon was perfectly capable of killing all three of them to fulfill his dark ambition. Quatermain knew that there would be no reasoning with Simon. He was hoping to fire a shot to wound Simon. However, anticipating Quatermain's plan, Simon had purposefully stepped to shift his position, so that Adisa stood between them. Quatermain silently cursed, and Simon was delighted to see the old man's frustration.

"I am sorry, did I throw off your aim?" Simon asked mockingly.

"The game is up, Simon. You have lost. There is no reason to take any more lives!" Quatermain pleaded, though he kept his hand tightly on the trigger.

"Even if you do manage to kill me... there are still a few things I want to take care of first..." Simon said to Quatermain, and then he looked at Adisa with intense hatred in his eyes and pulled the trigger.

Time seemed to slow as Quatermain watched Adisa fall forward in front of him, her arms outstretched as she hit the ground. Simon had already started to run, and Quatermain fired a shot. It passed clean through Simon's free arm, and hit one of the ropes on the rickety wooden bridge. Simon yelled in agony, and sprinted as swiftly as he could across the now swaying structure.

Quatermain rushed to Adisa's side, and immediately saw the severity of her wound. She only had moments to live, and was already coughing up blood, but she was trying to speak. He leaned in closer to hear her last words.

"My brother... please... save him... please..." was all that Adisa managed. Quatermain looked into her eyes and saw that same terror that he beheld in the marketplace. She was frightened for his life, and Quatermain gave her a solid, resolute nod. Adisa closed her eyes knowing that Quatermain would do everything in his power to save her brother.

Quatermain looked over to Ganizani, and saw that the detective was

"…a pained expression crossed Anthony's face…"

badly beaten. Though he was beginning to stir, Quatermain knew that it would be wasting time trying to revive Ganizani, and his injuries were too great for him to be of any assistance. Knowing that it was up to him alone to stop Simon, the great hunter charged across the bridge, hoping to catch him before he reached the other side.

In the distance, Quatermain could see Simon making his way along the bridge. Simon was putting a great strain on the structure as he pulled himself along the wooden planks, causing the entire bridge to sway and bend. Quatermain thought it best not to look down, lest fear prevent him from advancing. Simon stopped, as he felt Quatermain's own weight sway the bridge even further, and he turned to face the old hunter.

Simon took a shot at Quatermain. The swaying and unsteadiness of the bridge caused the bullet to fly harmlessly over Quatermain's shoulder. Quatermain had kept moving, and was thankful Simon had stopped, even if it was to shoot at him. Yet the consequence of this was that, while Quatermain gained on his target, Simon also had a much better chance of hitting Quatermain.

Quatermain would not give Simon the opportunity, and fired back at him. Hastily aimed, the shot was not intended to kill, or even hit the man, but rather to cause Simon to panic and lose his aim. In that, Quatermain succeeded, and Simon ducked and flinched, causing his next shot to go wild once more.

Now nearly thirty feet from his opponent, Quatermain was dismayed to discover that Simon had recovered, but instead of taking another shot at him, Simon had decided to run further along the bridge and onto solid ground. Quatermain sprinted as swiftly as he could, for the bridge afforded no cover. Suddenly, Simon turned to face him. His smug, mocking grin was gone, replaced with a stern, bitter expression.

"Goodbye, Quatermain."

Simon placed his pistol against one of the suspension ropes and fired! The bullet cut through the old, fragile rope like butter, causing one side of the bridge to give way! Quatermain reached out with his free arm and grabbed the ropes of the other side as the bridge bent and twisted wildly. Holding on for dear life, Quatermain watched as some of the boards plunged into the wild river below. If his grip loosened, even for a second, he would be joining them.

There were now only two ropes connecting the bridge, and Quatermain saw that Simon had aimed his pistol at the first one. If he fired, then Quatermain would sail back away from Simon to the other end of the chasm, thereby loosing his chance to apprehend the mastermind of this complex string of murders. Suddenly, Quatermain realized he had one possible route of escape, though he would be placing himself in even greater peril! Still, it was the only chance he had to succeed.

Time appeared to move slowly, almost at a glacial pace, as Quatermain swung his rifle arm towards the suspension rope at the other end of the bridge. Firing with at outstretched armed whilst being unable to look down the rifles' sights, was indeed the worst shooting conditions that anyone could ask for. Realizing that he only had one bullet left, Quatermain took the chance and fired!

The bullet struck the suspension rope at the opposite end of the bridge, causing the far end to swing free! Quatermain dropped the rifle and held on with all of his strength as the entire structure swung towards the cliff! The force of the reaction caused the rope Simon was aiming at to bend and twist, thus his shot harmlessly embedded itself into the wooden post. As Quatermain watched the cliff race towards him, he gritted his teeth and braced for impact. He soon felt the bridge shudder from the violent collision, and he gripped the boards with all the strength he had left to save himself.

Looking down would only paralyze him, but Quatermain knew that looking up did not present a pleasant alternative. Though he did not have much further to climb before he would be on solid ground, he knew that Simon was standing over him with a loaded weapon. Quatermain grimaced bitterly, realizing that his action seemed to only delay the inevitable. He made a tremendous effort to climb the planks, but he soon saw Simon's head cresting over the edge, an expression of fury and loathing on his face.

"You are one damnably frustrating old man to deal with!" Simon spat, leveling his pistol at Quatermain's head. Quatermain saw that it was only a few more feet to get on solid ground, but he dared not move. The great hunter's mind flashed back to other times, attempting to recall if he had survived a similar fate.

"How will you explain this away, Simon!" Quatermain barked, it was all that he could think to say.

Simon's face changed back to its customary smug smile. "Simple enough, Mr. Quatermain... senile adventurer, infatuated with Africa, forms an alliance with an empire-hating African detective and revives a cult of assassins... You see Mr. Quatermain, I have come this far because I plan for everything... every contingency."

"You have not planned for everything... you pull that trigger and your weapon misfires." Quatermain warned as he looked down the barrel of

Simon's pistol. It was then that he noticed the hammer was bent ever so slightly out of place. "You try to shoot me and your hand blows off!"

"What? This was working just fine moments ago... do you take me for a fool?"

"Killing Quatermain would be pointless!" Ganizani's voice echoed across the chasm. Simon looked from Quatermain to Ganizani, who stood at the edge of the precipice, shouting at him. "I too know the truth, Simon, and I'll have a warrant for your arrest!"

"And whose word do you think they will take? A well respected consulate, or a foolish, anti-colonial detective? I'm afraid that they will not listen." Simon said with satisfaction, as he glanced back down to Quatermain, but to his great shock, the hunter was gone! Ganizani's threat had distracted him, and Simon swore aloud, frustrated that he allowed himself to take his eye off his target.

Simon peered down into the churning waters below, but could see no indication of Quatermain's body on the rocks or in the stream. He did not recall hearing Quatermain scream either, so he assumed that the hunter had made his way onto land and was now more dangerous to him than ever. Quatermain must have swiftly and silent climbed up the side of the bridge to evade him. Feeling rage overtake his judgement, Simon impulsively went to fire his pistol at Ganizani, but then Quatermain's warning flashed into his mind. Had the old hunter been lying about the pistol to merely buy himself some time? Unable to decide, Simon kept the pistol in his hand as he trampled through the jungle to find Quatermain.

✺ ✺ ✺

However, finding a man such as Quatermain was a task much easier said than done. Though he was more frequently the hunter than the hunted, Quatermain had learned to cover his tracks and move stealthily through the terrain. Simon, though he was certainly formidable and no stranger to the jungle, could not have hoped to surprise Quatermain. The old hunter, despite being unarmed and defenseless, felt comfortable as he moved from various vantage points.

Despite being pursued by Simon, Quatermain had another matter on his mind: finding Adisa's brother. While he was hanging onto the remnants of the bridge, Quatermain was able to see Simon's boots, and he recognized the brand. In his time, Quatermain had learned not only to track animals, but people as well, and he noticed that Simon's footprints were already scattered throughout this part of the jungle. It was clear that Simon had been here before, and he saw the faintest trails of drag marks along the ground. The old hunter surmised that Simon had dragged Adisa's brother to this spot. Quatermain hoped that he could get to him in time.

Following the footprints, and knowing that Simon was still too far away to see or hear him, Quatermain made his way to a cave that was in the side of a rock face. It was well concealed by the trees and foliage, and most people would never have known of its existence. The cave would have been the ideal spot to hide a prisoner.

Stepping inside, Quatermain was thankful that some moon beams were shining into the cave from the opening and were bouncing off an underground pool, providing adequate illumination. He could hear the sounds of a young man moaning, and surmised that Adisa's brother had been given a dose of the same sedative that he was shot with earlier. Following the noise, Quatermain soon located the young man and examined him. He looked to be no older than seventeen, with wild black hair and a face that reflected his current torment. Adisa's brother looked at Quatermain with groggy eyes, and only had the energy to speak.

"Who... are you?" he said. It was the same dialect that Adisa had used, so Quatermain was able to hold a conversation with him.

"I am a friend of Adisa'. She sent me to get you out of here." Quatermain said as he examined the ropes tying the young man to a rock. Simon had been thorough, and tied him with several strands of rope to a large stalagmite protruding from the ground. Quatermain began to undo the first rope when Adisa's brother began to speak.

"You are... English... like the other man, Simon...." he said, trying to sort through his thoughts.

"I am English, but I am nothing like Simon. I am trying to rescue you from him. What is your name?" Quatermain said while he worked on the ropes. To Quatermain's chagrin, Simon had used sailor's knots, and he had wished he was carrying a machete or other blade to make quick work of them. Alas, time was not on his side, and the knots were exceedingly difficult to untie in the dark.

"Jabari..." he said faintly.

"Listen to me, Jabari. Simon is hunting me, and odds are that he will probably come back here to see if I have found you." Quatermain said as he worked at the knots. Jabari was becoming more focused, and his thoughts were more coherent.

"Where is Adisa? How is she?" Jabari asked. Quatermain's pained expression told the young man all that he needed to know, and his eyes began to well up with tears.

"I'm sorry, Jabari... Simon killed her. Her last wish was for me to rescue you." Quatermain said, hoping that Jabari would find some comfort knowing that his sister's last thoughts were of protecting him. Jabari said nothing, but Quatermain could hear him softly weeping. With the knots undone, the young man attempted to stand up, but stumbled back to the ground. Quatermain gave him a shoulder to lean on, and began to look around the cave. Jabari broke his silence with the words:

"I will kill him." He spoke plainly and simply.

"You're in no condition to fight," Quatermain cautioned as he looked around the cave. "Simon will come back here—most likely to finish you off because you're not needed anymore. We have to hide you."

"I'm strong enough!" Jabari protested as his body shook. As the sedative wore off, he was once again feeling the pain of the beatings that Simon had inflicted on him. Quatermain watched him shudder and wince.

"No, you're not." Quatermain said bluntly as he helped Jabari move to a safer location. Around the edge of the lake was a small mound of stalagmites. The moonlight did not reach that area, and finding Jabari would have been difficult, if not impossible. Quatermain knew that he had to distract Simon to keep Jabari safe, but how? He began to search the cave for an improvised weapon, but to his horror, he saw the silhouette of Simon standing at the cave entrance, the moon behind him.

"Quatermain... what have you done with the boy?" Simon asked, seeing that Jabari was not there. His pistol was leveled at Quatermain as he walked into the cave, causing the old hunter to slowly step back.

"He is safe... and far from here." Quatermain spoke clearly, his voice echoing throughout the cave.

"I doubt that... he could barely walk after what I did to him." Simon sneered as he looked around the cave. "You have hidden him somewhere. Very well, I'll just have to hunt the little runt down and finish him off!"

"You might as well put that gun away, Simon. I've told you that it is useless now." Quatermain cautioned, only to get scoffed at by Simon.

"Mr. Quatermain, you are a great hunter, but a terrible liar." Simon said before turning his head to yell. "I'll kill you, you little runt! Just like I killed your sister!"

Jabari, with a tremendous effort, sprung from behind his cover and lobbed a rock at Simon! Due to his pain and deliriousness, the rock flew far over Simon's head and bounced off against a larger stalactite, loosening it.

Simon instinctively aimed and shot at Jabari. Instead of shooting Jabari, the weapon exploded in his hand! The deafening noise reverberated through the cave, and the stalactite went crashing to the earth! It was the last thing that Simon saw as he looked up.

Quatermain raced over to Jabari and hoisted him up. Several of the smaller stalactites had come loose and were falling to the ground as well. The two raced outside the cave and looked back as the dust was beginning to settle.

"Damned fool... he should have listened to me!" Quatermain grimaced as he watched the rising dust.

"I have killed a man..." Jabari said, trying to catch his breath.

"Adisa has been avenged, Jabari." Quatermain said plainly, helping the young man get into a sitting position.

"Simon... the Night's Hand... too much blood has been spilled," Jabari mused.

"I suppose you are the leader of the Night's Hand now," Quatermain said.

"Then I will disband them. We have become the servants of evil... and I do not wish to have that be my family's legacy."

Quatermain smiled, proud of Jabari's wisdom. "There is a detective in the city that I need you to speak with, and then this whole affair will finally be over."

✾ ✾ ✾

Quatermain sat in Ganizani's office as the detective transcribed his version of the events. Per his usual fashion, Quatermain would attempt to downplay his part in the adventure, being loath to admit that his actions were the catalyst for solving the murders. Ganzani would periodically interrupt Quatermain with a question. The statement given by Jabari, coupled with the trail of evidence that Simon left behind, closed the case to the satisfaction of the English government.

"And what happened to the flute in Henry Trasker's room?" Ganizani asked.

"I would guess that Adisa snuck in and retrieved it. If people suspected a connection with the flutes, she would never be able to sell them." Quatermain surmised.

"I see... and how long did you suspect that Simon was behind the whole affair?" the detective asked, looking up from his notes. Quatermain hesitated before answering.

"Not to boast, but I suspected him from the meeting in his office, after I had apprehended the first assassin," Quatermain said with a small, gentle shrug.

"What did he do to... to put you on his track, so to speak?"

"It was nothing he did," Quatermain admitted, "but like any hunter, you must pay attention to your environment. I had noticed that he had a small but impressive library on African folklore and culture... which I thought was unusual for a man who seemed to look down upon the native people. I think you will find that the Night's Hand are mentioned in several of the texts he owns... and that those pages have been subtly earmarked."

"But... and I must play devil's advocate, it is possible that he may have believed your story and attempted to investigate the Night's Hand himself," Ganizani said interested to see what Quatermain's response would be.

"I had considered that... except that the first assassin I encountered had said something that troubled me."

"Which was?"

"He called me... Mr. Quatermain. I know that this may seem like a small matter, and perhaps I am reading too much into this... but historically the Night's Hand have been a separatist, secretive tribe. Learning to speak English would only have been a priority of the chieftains, being necessary on matters of business. So why would an assassin not refer to me by my more common African name of Macumazahn? He must have known of me, and been told by an English source what my Christian name was." Quatermain said, recalling the incident.

"And we now know that Simon himself murdered the assassin." Ganizani said, remembering the bewilderment he felt when his men found the assassin's dead body in the cell.

"Yes, that is why he was running late for his meeting with me. No one thought to question his presence in the police station, and he was able to slip the assassin a vial of poison, and then he planted those sandals with the rest of the garbage to frame you, Detective Granizani. Simon Grint was a clever and evil man," Quatermain surmised, starting to feel weary. This adventure had tired him considerably, and he fantasized about lying on a cot in the shade.

"Yes indeed... all this blood... for money and power," Ganizani sighed.

"There will always be men like Simon... and men like you to keep them in check, detective." Quatermain stood up, feeling that the conversation was drawing to a close. The two shook hands, both feeling a hard-won mutual respect for each other.

"And what about men like you, Mr. Quatermain?"
Quatermain shrugged as he closed the door.

THE END

WRITING A CLASSIC HERO

The most interesting aspect of Allan Quatermain, I feel, is his humility. Though he can accurately be considered the Indiana Jones of his time, the two are vastly different in terms of character. Many film versions of Quatermain have attempted to make use of his namesake in order to provide their audience with the same type of thrills as Indiana Jones, but neglected to give the character a different personality. However, since they were copying Jones, they also attempted to put his personality into Quatermain, and I did my best to make him true to the hero we were introduced to in the novel "King Solomon's Mines".

I was admittedly stuck mid-way through the story, and after taking a break from it for a while, I realized that my main problem was that I had confined Quatermain, a naturalist and hunter, to the city. Quickly fixing that problem, I had great fun constructing various death traps and escapes for our hero. Each time I would describe the situation aloud to a friend of loved one, I noticed that I would keep adding elements to get an even bigger reaction from my captive audience. Eventually, I had to draw the line at some point, and there were oftentimes where I would think of a situation that would have been impossible to escape: period! But, these are the things I love about pulps, and I hoped to create some memorable moments.

Going into this story, beyond doing the research on Quatermain, I also had to research African and English history. What I found was an interesting dynamic between the African police and the English officials, so I decided to incorporate that into my story. Another personal preference of mine is to have my heroic characters use their brains in place of their fists, thus the invention of Detective Ganizani. Indeed, many of the African names in the story were convenient ways to characterize them once I found the meaning of each name.

In all honesty, I was not sure how the story was going to end when I sat down to write it. As I was typing and learning more about Adisa, I realized that the cliché of the assassin with a code of honor was, in my opinion, an oxymoron. If one were indeed truly honorable, they would not become a killer in the first place. I knew, however, that Simon was going to be my villain, and one of my favorite moments in fiction is when villains butt-heads. Therefore, having the two of them argue about this was an interesting concept for me, and in that moment I decided to make Adisa more sympathetic than I originally intended. Hopefully the readers will be slightly surprised, because I sure was when I got there!

Although I would say this story is more about an investigation than an actual mystery, I hope that there is enough here to keep the reader interested and guessing. Quatermain is a unique hero among the ones at Airship 27 and I am glad to have been given a chance to write for this great adventurer!

❀ ❀ ❀

ERIK FRANKLIN - is a writer/actor/filmmaker based in Seattle. Recently graduating with honors from the Art Institute of Seattle in film production, he is the co-President of Franklin-Husser Entertainment LLC. He is working on two upcoming feature films for his company: A dinosaur action film "Revenge of the Lost" and the martial arts comedy "3 Morons Fighting Ninja". You can give the company page a "Like" at: https://www.facebook.com/pages/Franklin-Husser-Entertainment-LLC/290795021042906.

Drawn to pulp fiction through his love of history, literature, and Americana, he is grateful for Airship 27 Productions giving him the opportunity to write his first story. He looks forward to writing more adventures!

STONES OF BLOOD
BY ALAN J. PORTER

NOVEMBER 1880

The coppery tang of fresh blood in the air reached the nostrils of the hunter. They would be gathering soon, and he knew where to find them. The trail was one he hadn't trod in many years, but it still remained familiar, even in the early predawn gloom. Few men ventured out at this hour, but he welcomed the dark. His highly tuned senses seemed to be particular suited to nocturnal activities. Besides in this place the sounds and smells of the daylight hours could be almost overwhelming.

He let the last few hours of the darkness enfold him and followed the scent of the fresh blood towards his destination, where he knew he would be welcomed. Within minutes he sighted his quarry stood next to its kill. A man, fresh blood splatters coating his ritual white garments, proudly stood next to the dismembered carcass of a beast that had then been cleaved in two, each half now swinging from a wooden beam like a pair of grisly trophies. In his hand the man held a heavy blade from which drops of blood fell and pooled on the floor by his feet.

The man turned and caught sight of the hunter as he approached from the shadows. The bloody implement was raised, pointing in the direction of the new arrival. There it stayed for several seconds as the butcher sized up the hunter and decided what his next move should be. Suddenly the deadly weapon flew in a downward arc and was embedded with a loud thump in a nearby wooden stump.

The butcher's firm countenance broke in to a grin, and he threw his arms wide in welcome, "My god, Quatermain, is that you, you old dog?"

Allan Quatermain stepped into his friend's welcoming embrace, "Good to see you too, William."

The two men broke apart, and the butcher grasped the hunter by the shoulder, "What's powerful enough to bring you out of your jungle to this one?"

Quatermain smiled and gave just a single word in response, "Harry."

"Your boy?"

Quatermain nodded, and changed the subject; "You seem to have found a new calling my old friend."

The butcher smiled, "Slaughtering animals for food rather than sport may not be as lucrative, but it's steady work and I guess it makes me a respectable business man now." He pointed up at the facade of the building behind him, which bore the painted legend of *Wm. Burroughs Esq. Butcher. Smithfield Market* above the doorway. "How long will you be in town for?"

"Just long enough to get Harry settled into his medical studies."

"So your lad's going to be a doctor."

"That's his wish."

"So why make your first stop in London a visit to your old pal rather than with your flesh and blood?"

"I'll be meeting him for breakfast soon enough, but first I wanted to start the day with something a bit more to my tastes. Family obligations might take me out of the jungle, but..."

William Burroughs smiled. "... you can't take the jungle out of you. I know the feeling. It took me a long time to acclimatize to so called civilization. I have just the thing you need. Come on in."

Allan Quatermain smiled ruefully to himself as he descended the wide stairway towards the lower level of the ornately decorated restaurant that his son had selected for their rendezvous. The establishment had been easy to find, located just to one side of the cobbled plaza that fronted the Covent Garden Market, filled with its mix of farmers' stalls, flower girls, and street performers; whilst among them strolled a mix of tradesmen and well dressed theater lovers who had clearly enjoyed the overnight delights of the nearby theater district. The stairs descended towards a private bar area and split about two thirds of the way down with a choice of left or right curved paths instead of, what Quatermain thought would be a much more useful, straight descent. The hunter took the left hand route, for no particular reason beyond that he had observed that given such a choice most people went right; going left also meant he would be in more open space and freer to observe; although truth be told there wasn't much to observe beyond the few tables at which sat some of the aforementioned theater patrons, and the occasional pairing of businessmen deep in serious conversation. The restaurant may have only been a thirty minute walk from Smithfileds but the contrast was profound, they could have been two different worlds, and Quatermain knew which one he preferred.

Harry was sat at a small table for two off to the left hand side of the restaurant; he stood and lifted his arm in a combination of greeting and recognition as he spotted his father descending the staircase. He motioned to the empty seat opposite him, and Quatermain strode over and stood by it. He was stunned. He didn't know what to do. What was the correct protocol in these circumstances? He didn't normally care too much for polite society or its cultural nuances; he normally just acted the way he felt he wanted to; but in this instance he didn't want to do anything that might cause his son embarrassment. Was it okay for him to throw his arms around his son in a warming paternal bear hug, or would a simple formal shake of the hands suffice? In the end he did neither. A short nod of the head, followed by a brief "Harry," was delivered before he took his seat.

"Father" came the equally brief reply as Harry reseated himself. "I hope you don't mind, but I've already ordered for both of us. I assume it's been a while since you've had a traditional full English breakfast meal."

Quatermain thought back to his earlier repast with Burroughs. He doubted they'd serve anything like that in a place like this, and it definitely couldn't be described as traditional, so he smiled and agreed, "It certainly has."

At first conversation between the two men was sparse and awkward, neither being comfortable with the practice of small talk. It was something of a relief when the plates arrived, Quatermain had to admit that the combination of eggs, bacon, grilled tomatoes, mushrooms and black pudding was surprisingly tasty. The practice of lightly burning bread to make toast was not one he approved of, and so left that aside. With food in their stomachs the father and son relaxed and the dialog flowed freer over several cups of coffee that had accompanied and followed the meal. They talked of Quatermain's life in Africa, but only in the abstract as he refused to share details of his exploits, even with his own son; but mostly they talked of Harry's plans to join the medical profession.

"Would you like to see my digs?" Harry suddenly asked. "You have no idea where I live, and I'd like you to have some idea of how I spend my days ... and your money." He chuckled at his own addendum. "Come on," he stood without waiting for an answer. The bill had already been paid and he was clearly anxious to set off.

Despite the incessant background drone of the theater goers and the businessmen's conversations in the high ceiling room, the restaurant had been a comparative oasis of quiet calm compared with the noise that assailed their ears on leaving. As they stepped through the front door Quatermain was reacquainted with the sound of one of the busiest spots in the city of London. Stall holders hawking their wares each competing to be louder than their compatriots, tradesman bartering, the almost songlike lilt of the flower girls, the horses' hooves and the steel rimmed carriage wheels drumming out a slow rumble on the stone cobbles of the surrounding streets. But above all that rose a few sounds that Quatermain hadn't heard on his previous crossing of the plaza on the way the restaurant. The incessant clack-clack-clack of a wooden rattle, a police rattle designed to call for assistance. It was accompanied by the sounds of heavy foot falls and big boots with metal studs sparking off the stone streets. A shout of "Stop!" struggled to be heard over the general melee.

"Look out!" It was Harry's voice.

Quatermain turned and found himself face to face with a large well-muscled man running towards him at full speed with a small canvas bag tucked under his arm. A second man followed closely by, a blade dripping blood held in his right hand. Ten yards behind them came the policeman, who was gripping his side in some distress with one hand, while spinning his rattle with the other.

"Move granddad!" The big man growled as he bore down on Quatermain.

Quatermain moved.

But not in the way that the big man anticipated. Instead of moving back to let the runner pass, Allan Quatermain stepped forward to face him. He let the runner's momentum carry him towards him and as the man reached him he turned sideways on, reaching out his arm straight as a barrier. The locked arm caught the runner under the chin and the big man pirouetted around Quatermain's arm before falling on his back on the cobbles with a heavy thump violent enough to drive the breath from his body. The canvas bag flew from his arms and landed a few feet away. The second man was on Quatermain in seconds, the blade he carried now raised in a posture of attack. He thrust it forward at Quatermain's face. The hunter ducked his head to one side, and without changing his stance reached up and grabbed the man's wrist, he bent it back and the joint's bones surrendered to the unnatural movement with a loud crack. The knife spun away to land near the canvas bag, while its former owner sank to the pavement howling in agony.

"Thank you," the wounded police man reached Quatermain's side, and his pursuit over, slowly sank to his knees. Before Quatermain could say anything his son was at the law officer's side, his cravat removed and used to stanch the flow of blood from the knife puncture in the man's side. A second and third officer soon arrived from the other side of the market square and quickly tried to take control of the small crowd starting to gather around the prostrate villains. Stepping over the still wheezing big man, Quatermain reached down, picked up the knife, and grinned at the man on the floor. "Lets see what this was all about, shall we?" He placed the tip of the blade against the bag and flicked his wrist rendering a neat slice through the canvas. A small stream of stones trickled out on to the cobbles. Allan Quatermain reached down and picked up one, turning it slowly between thumb and forefinger. He instantly recognized what the plunder had been. "Uncut diamonds," he murmured to himself, "how interesting."

✿ ✿ ✿

"Interested, Mr. Quatermain?" The imposing figure in the frock coat rose from behind his ornate, and equally imposing, carved mahogany desk, dipped the nib of the pen in an ivory inkwell fashioned from the end of an elephant tusk, and offered the pen towards Quatermain. "All you have to do is sign, and it's a done deal."

Quatermain stared at the inkwell and couldn't help but wonder if he'd had some part in its journey from animal to desk. He refocused on the proffered writing instrument and the quarto page of legalese that lay before him. Things had moved fast, even by his standards; he was used to being drawn into adventures at seemingly the slightest provocation, but it had been less than an hour since breakfast, and already he felt his world changing. Allan Quatermain may have been a man of adventure, able to deal with whatever the jungle threw a him, but in his fifty odd years of existence on the planet he'd also come to realize that underneath the turmoil of the adventurer and hunter he liked some resemblance of stability. He'd come to London to see his son, nothing more; yet now even that simple task was about to be complicated by his reputation.

"You say that this agreement will protect Harry's future?" Quatermain asked of the man behind the desk.

"DeBeers always takes care of its obligations." The man seemed almost insulted by the fact that Quatermain had asked the question, but hid his displeasure behind the stereotypical stoic reserve of the English establishment. "If you won't take a payment for yourself, then we are happy to provide a steady stream of funds for your son until such time as he has set himself up as a medical professional."

"Covering all his tuition and living fees while studying and the costs of his first year of practice."

"As discussed."

With the affirmation of the deal he'd negotiated with the diamond merchants, Quatermain accepted the pen and signed his name to the document in question. "So where do I start in tracking down your diamond thieves?"

The man behind the desk smiled, "I suggest that you start by having a conversation with The Young Detective."

Quatermain looked at the street name on the note that the man from DeBeers had handed him as he left the office. He looked up and checked the name again against the plaque on the street corner building. It was a match. But there was no sign of anyone on the street who matched the description he'd been given. His keen eyes scanned the passersby a second time, and a third, but with no result.

"You won't find me there, Mr. Quatermain."

The voice had come from directly behind him, even though he had sensed no-one at his back. Quatermain spun and quickly sized up the speaker. He was a tall thin, maybe too thin, young man in his mid-twenties, with hawkish features and all-seeing eyes. His dress was functional but not as stylish as you would expect for a man of his age; it was also marked with scruffs and odd traces of plaster dust. "Been in a bit of a scuffle have we?" remarked Quatermain.

"Very good." the young man acknowledged. "And how may I assist the great Elephant Hunter?"

"Are you sure you are addressing the right man?"

"Please," the young man seemed exasperated, "must we do this." He paused. "A man in his early fifties, leathery well tanned skin from an outdoor life, and from the tone of the tan, one spent in Africa. You are well muscled, but not overly so, exceptionally fit for a man your age, but you don't hold yourself like a military man. You are constantly checking out your surroundings, and you stand on the balls of your feet ready for action. Therefore a hunter, and as I was told to meet Allan Quatermain, and elephant hunter of considerable repute at this very spot, it must be you."

Quatermain nodded in acquiescence. "Why meet here, it's a busy place for a sensitive conversation."

The young detective smiled, "Sometimes the greatest privacy is to be had in the most crowded of places. Besides I was in the area; looking at potentially renting a suite of rooms in a property on this street. I believe I may have found the perfect location; the landlady seems very amenable, with a few secrets of her own."

"So what do you know about diamonds, young man?"

"A considerable amount," it wasn't a boast Quatermain noted, simply a statement of fact. "The reason DeBeers suggested that you seek my assistance is due to the fact that they commissioned me to produce a paper for them on the differences in chemical composition of specimens produced from their various mines."

"Wouldn't they know that themselves?"

"The findings of the geologists they have on staff were rudimentary at best, I merely provided them with clarification."

Quatermain reached into his pocket and drew out a small stone; a sample from the robbery that he had foiled that morning and provided by DeBeers, on loan of course, to use during his enquires. He passed the stone over to the detective. "So where does this one come from?"

The young man, rolled it over in his palm, then looked straight into Quatermain's gaze and smiled. "Why it's from The Dog and Duck of course."

🌿 🌿 🌿

"What I don't understand," The young man said as they walked across the threshold of the aforementioned public house, "is this strange fascination that so many have with polished chunks of carbon."

The remark caught Quatermain off guard as the last hour, as they had strolled from the corner of Baker Street to Westminster, had passed in silence. It took the hunter a beat to pick up that the young man was essentially continuing their previous conversation. He coughed as a quick stalling tactic as he tried to recall the last exchange, "I must admit, neither have I," he agreed, "but that fascination has proven to be highly lucrative over the years. So I'm not complaining."

The pub had a narrow facade of black wood with gold pinstriping, it looked clean and well maintained. On the right hand door frame there were several small plaques representing various regimental coats of arms on display. Quatermain nodded towards the plaques, "Army pub?"

"Correct," the detective acknowledged.

"So why do you think that uncut diamond came from here?"

"Because the man you so ably apprehended this morning is a trooper with the 60th Rifles, and this is their regular watering hole when they are barracked in the city."

Quatermain nodded, "I guess that's as good a reason as any. Let's head on in then."

In keeping with the narrow frontage the interior was equally lacking in width. The bar ran along the right hand wall with just enough floor space in front for patrons to stand no more than two or three deep. Making it feel even more cramped was a casement for a set of wrought iron stairs on the left. A hand written chalk board notice indicated that the stairs up to the floor above gave access to a 'Private Dining Room —Available for Functions Upon Request.' Tucked under the casement was another opening that hinted at a set of wooden steps leading to a basement. Sounds of laughter, shouting, and the occasional snatches of song filtered up from below. The detective pointed down, Quatermain nodded again. He didn't like being lead around like this. He was the tracker and hunter, but this wasn't his territory. He may not have been comfortable, but he knew when to let those with local knowledge point the way. The stairs were very narrow, little more than shoulder width, and steep. A rough well splintered door barred the bottom of the staircase. The detective gave it a gentle push, it wasn't locked. It swung open into what was clearly the pub's basement, but which with the addition of some rustic tables, chairs, and wooden benches had been transformed into a rudimentary tap room. Hanging from the exposed rafters were tattered flags, and pinned to the walls were jackets, helmets, weapons, and other souvenirs of various military engagements on foreign soil.

"Can I help you Gentlemen?" The question was polite, but the undertone was threatening. Quatermain tensed and rose to the balls of his feet. The detective must have sensed the movement, for he, almost imperceptibly shook his head and addressed the speaker, a large man with a well trimmed and cultivated set of whiskers. "Thank you Sergeant. My name is Sherlock Holmes, and my companion here," he gestured in Quatermain's direction," Is the renowned hunter, Mr. Allan Quatermain. We'd like to ask you about Trooper Davis."

"Are those names meant to impress me? 'Cause I ain't heard of neither of you. As for Davis, the boy was an idiot, got himself arrested this morning."

"Yes, we know," the detective replied and pointed back at the still tense Quatermain, "and this is the gentleman that apprehended him."

The Sergeant looked Quatermain up and down. "From what we 'eard it was a nice move that clobbered the idiot. He was a strong lad too. My apologies, but I hadn't imagined a man of your years capable of the deed."

Quatermain just smiled.

"So what was he doing?"

"Running stolen diamonds," Quatermain spoke. The general hub-bub of the tap room fell instantly silent.

"Got what he deserved then."

"That he did, Sergeant." Holmes agreed. "Did he have any particular friends here that he may have confided in?"

"A drinking buddy you mean?" The Sergeant paused. "Mills, Trooper Davey Mills."

"And where would we find Trooper Mills?"

The Sergeant turned and addressed the room in general, the consensus was that Trooper Mills, like Trooper Davis before his dramatic entrance earlier that morning, hadn't been seen for several days, not since they'd all been issued a four-day pass.

"Hang on," said the Sergeant, "he likes those animals, the ones we saw in Africa on our last posting."

"Regent's Park Zoo. Thank you Sargent. We'll be on our way."

"One thing before you go. How did you know I was a Sergeant. I'm not in uniform."

"Tricks of the trade," A few minutes after leaving the pub Holmes turned to Quatermain and asked, "Did you notice something odd about the soldiers in there?"

Quatermain answered, "You mean that a lot of them seemed to have either recent scars, or were wounded in some way."

"You can keep your cobbled streets and alleyways, your public houses and hansom cabs, and the smell of human filth and horse dung," Allan Quatermain took a deep breath as they entered the zoo, "This is my territory; or at least as close to it as I'll ever find in this squalid metropolis."

"So where do we start to find our elusive Trooper?" Holmes asked, somewhat superciliously.

Quatermain ignored the implied barb, and flatly stated,"Springbok." His companion looked at him momentarily puzzled. "South Africa. The Sergeant said they had been stationed there and he liked the animals. The Springbok deer is plentiful and would most easily remind him of those times."

"In that case," the young detective acknowledged with a nod of the head, "lead on."

The two arrived at the relevant enclosure to find that they were the sole audience to a herd of deer that were happily grazing oblivious, or uncaring, of the fact that they were under observation. Immediately the younger man started scanning the scene. Within a minute he let out a triumphant "Ah Ha!" and ran his hand along the top of the enclosure's stone wall. Raising his hand he displayed a couple of cotton threads held in the precise grip of his long thin fingers. "Our man has been here or at least someone from the same regiment, for these threads match the color and density of the regimental jacket of the 60th Rifles. He pointed to a small black mark at the base of the wall, "and here he scraped the toe of his boots, for this is military grade polish."

"Why would he be in uniform?" Quatermain asked, "None of the others in the public house wore their regimental dress."

"It would suggest that he was on his way to an official appointment with another member of the regiment, a senior officer perhaps?"

"You may have proved that a member of the 60th stopped here, but how do we know it was Trooper Mills?"

The detective once more indicated the top of the wall. "A small blood stain, relatively recent, and from the position and length I'd say it suggested a wound on the right forearm."

"Sounds like it could be him," Quatermain paused, and slowly turned through a complete circle before returning his gaze to his companion. "You may have proven that our quarry was in fact here, and not too long ago. Now let me show you how to find out where he has gone. The time for detection is past, now we must become hunters." Quatermain moved past a slightly startled Holmes, who wasn't used to others taking the lead, and began heading down a side path, his pace quickening as he went. Almost like a hound catching the scent of the fox, he was after his quarry. For the first time the young detective observed the true aspect of the legend that was Allan Quatermain. So far he had felt constrained by the unnatural surroundings of the city as if its narrow streets and tall buildings were physically holding him at bay, but now the apparent years fell away and the man became the myth. He moved with the grace of a panther, and the speed of a cheetah; so much so that the younger man almost had difficulty in keeping up. He seemed to be constantly testing his senses, sniffing, and even tasting, the air as they moved. The head in constant motion listening and scanning his surroundings. Fingers reaching out to caress leaf fronds

"Our man has been here…"

and branches as they passed. The direction changes were quick and sudden yet always gave the impression that they had been planned well in advance. Towards the end of one of the paths Quatermain came to an abrupt stop, and silently signaled his companion to halt. He held his arm out to the right and pointed gesturing for the detective to take a side path. The two separated and taking the divergent paths circled around to enter the spectator area in front of the lion enclosure from either side. Standing between them was a young man in the regimental uniform of a Trooper of the 60th Rifles, his arm in a sling.

"Trooper Davey Mills" Holmes' declaration wasn't a question to confirm the man's identity, it was a statement of certainty. The Trooper spun to look in the detective's direction, then panicked and bolted in the opposite direction, right into the vise like grip of Allan Quatermain. The detective walked slowly towards the trapped man but ignored him and instead addressed himself to the hunter, "You must teach me to track a man like that. It is a skill that will provide dividends in the years to come."

"What do yah want?" the trapped soldier stopped struggling and directed his annoyance at the younger man.

"We believe that you are acquainted with Trooper Davis?"

"What of it?"

"He was arrested this morning."

"Nuthin' to do with me."

"Really." The detective paused, "Sorry to see you were injured in the line of duty."

The Trooper shrugged "It 'appens."

"A battle field wound I take it." The detective continued.

"Yep," the Trooper nodded, and added, "Caught a ball in the arm on my last tour." He sounded almost proud of the fact, like the wound was a badge of honor.

Quatermain adjusted his grip and suddenly moved his arm down grasping the Trooper's lower arm and squeezed right over the wound. The man yelped. Fresh blood seeped onto the bandage. "Still not healed after all this time?" Quatermain noted, "Yet you've been back in England for at least a fortnight according to the newspaper reports of troop movements. I'd say that was a recent wound."

"You bastard," The Trooper grimaced at the pain, "Regimental surgeon had to go back in and fix some'at."

"What would that be?" asked Holmes.

"'Ow would I bleedin' know?" The Trooper remained indignant." Why don't you ask 'im yourselves."

"I fully intend to. I surmise that you were perhaps on your way to an appointment with said gentleman; perhaps you would be kind enough to let us accompany you."

"Do I have any choice?" The Trooper asked.

"No." Quatermain responded as he released the soldier. "And don't think about making a bolt for it, I'll be on you before you get two paces."

"Somehow, I believe yah," Trooper Mills rubbed his injured arm.

The ninety minute train ride to Winchester, home of the 60th Rifles barracks, passed without incident; however Quatermain couldn't help notice the way that the young detective kept staring at the trooper's injured arm. In the end his curiosity as to his companion's behavior overcame any reticence to speak out. "Why are you so intent on the man's wound?"

"Today's encounter has made me realize that I have a serious gap in my knowledge of the effects that violence has on the human body."

"You have some strange obsessions," Quatermain observed.

His companion smiled and added as explanation; "I have an extensive knowledge of the effects of physical contact from fists, bare knuckle or with brass dusters, coshes, the effects and marks of strangulation, kicks, as well as various wounds from street weapons such as knives of various design, axes, cleavers such as those used by your butcher friend, and even various household objects used as weapons; but it is now apparent that I have no practical knowledge of the marks that military service and combat wounds can leave on a man. I need to rectify that."

"Why not just ask the sort of man we are currently on our way to meet?"

"Are you suggesting that I engage an army surgeon as a consultant to assist me as needed?"

"Why not, you can't know everything."

"But, I can know more than most."

"It was just a suggestion." Quatermain concluded the conversation and the fell back into mutually agreeable silence until they arrived at their destination.

Trooper Mills lead the way to the barrack gates where he spoke for the first time since they had left London. "Hang on 'ere a mo' while I let 'em know I'm 'ere to see the Doc."

"If you don't mind we'll accompany you."

"Suit yourselves," he grumbled. "They won't let you in without the

Doc's say so anyways." Mills approached the guard house, and spoke with familiarity to the Trooper on duty. "Hey 'arry. I'm here to see Doc Young 'bout me arm, like he asked."

"Hang on there, Danny," the guard answered, taking a sideways look at Quatermain and Holmes, clearly wondering who his comrade's companions were.

After a few minutes waiting a young officer appeared out of the guard house and approached them. He ignored Mills and approached Quatermain, assuming that as the elder man he was in charge of the party, "How may I be of assistance, sir?"

"We were hoping to meet with the Regimental Surgeon, a Doctor Young I believe. Trooper Mills here," he indicated the wounded solider, "was kind enough to suggest that we accompany him on his appointment." The Trooper snorted in derision at this statement.

"My I inquire as to the nature of your business with the Surgeon?" The officer asked.

"This may explain." The detective handed over a carte d'visite which the officer accepted turned over and read. Quatermain had never seen the card and no idea what it said, but it had an immediate effect on the officer whose eyes visibly widened. Handing it back he coughed, "I'm afraid you gentlemen are a couple of days late, Doctor Stephen Young volunteered to make an early return to the regiment still stationed in Africa."

"Thank you," responded the detective pocketing the card and turning to Quatermain added, "It seems that you may need to return home, my friend."

DECEMBER 1880

Several times during the long voyage back to Africa, Quatermain had thought about that card and what it had said, but the detective would not tell him anything beyond the enigmatic response that he had been given the card by his brother who did something or other in government circles. As well as provoking a startled response from the young officer at the gate it had also precipitated a meeting with the regimental commander. The senior officer confirmed Doctor Young's return to active duty, and provided Quatermain with his own personal orders. Orders that promised him the full assistance and cooperation of any member of the regiment he may encounter. Quatermain had spent the last few minutes re-examining that slip of paper while the cargo ship he had secured passage on docked. As soon as he felt the bump of the ship nudging against the rope bumpers hanging over the wharf's edge he folded the Commander's note and slipped it into his jacket pocket. Grabbing his pack from the bunk, he left his cabin and stepped on to the deck under bright South African sun. He let the rays soak in to his skin for a few moments, revitalizing him after the choking smoke-filled air of London, before heading over to the gangplank leading him down to the Cape Town dockside.

The soldier waiting at the foot of the gangplank introduced himself as Adjutant Lieutenant John Holloway in a broad Midlands accent that seemed at odds with his decidedly upper class rank and title. The Adjutant punctuated his introduction with a smart clipped salute before offering his hand. Ignoring it for a moment, Quatermain examined the man in front of him, he was shorter than he expected for a regimental officer. He surmised that the soldier must have stood on tiptoes to even get close to the minimum regulation regimental height requirements. Holloway was also more rotund than any of the other members of the 60th Rifles that he'd encountered to date. Quatermain's conclusion was that this man must be an exceptional soldier to have not only achieved his rank, but retained his commission given his distinctly non-regulation physical make-up. Someone had bent the rules for this man, and Quatermain wanted to know why. He held out his own hand in greeting. Holloway's grip was exceptionally strong, almost at the same levels as the hunter's own.

"No point in us standin' around 'ere all day," Holloway smiled. "I understand that youse wants to see a mine. An' not just any mine, but the biggest hole in the ground in these parts."

"Correct," Quatermain nodded. "I believe the company cabled ahead to set up an appointment with their agent on site."

"That'll be that fellah, Newman."

"Charles Newman."

"Shifty bugger that 'un." Holloway paused and looked at Quatermain as if trying to judge if the man had been offended by his forthright opinions. Quatermain's expression remained impassive, so Holloway continued, "Don't know how he got that posting; I wouldn't trust 'im as far as I could chuck 'im."

"Any particular reason?" asked Quatermain.

"Nah. I jus' don't like 'im." And with that Holloway picked up Quatermain's bags and marched off in the direction of the waiting horses. "No more fancy boats or trains from this point on, it's all horse back."

"Thanks goodness," Quatermain declared. "I've had enough of mechanical contraptions for a while."

The mine in question nestled near the junction of the Vaal and Orange Rivers in the area known as Griqualand West, about nine days ride north of Cape Town. Although it was nominally a British Territory, it had been the subject of on-going territorial disputes over the decade since diamonds had been discovered there. Prior to that no-one had cared about where Griqula tribesmen and their grazing herds roamed, but now they were prepared to go to war over those same lands, all for a hole in the ground that produced shiny rocks.

Allan Quatermain had to admit that on first impressions he had to agree with Lt. Holloway's assessment of Charles Newman. There was just something about the diamond merchant's agent that made you instinctively mistrust him. The man was tall, probably about six feet three inches Quatermain estimated, and he unnecessarily accentuated his height with the type of stove pipe hat made famous by the late American President. Newman was also incredibly thin, almost cadaverous with a pale skin that had failed to show any effects of being outside in the South African sun for prolonged periods. His eyes were permanently downcast, refusing to make contact with anyone who engaged him in conversation. His handshake was limp, his palm's clammy. There was nothing about the man's appearance of demeanor that invoked a sense of confidence.

"Welcome to camp, Mr. Quatermain. I have been expecting you for some weeks now." Newman's voice was low, almost a whisper. "The office in London ordered me to offer you every courtesy." He stopped as if carefully considering his next words, "Although they failed to divulge the purpose of your visit. A situation I find most disturbing."

"There's nothing sinister in my presence here, Mr. Newman. I'm here just to learn."

"And what can the Dark Continent's most famous elephant hunter and adventurer need to learn about diamond mining?" Newman paused as if for dramatic effect, "You see I know who you are; your reputation precedes you, and I fail to see how we can add to that by anything you may find out here. This is simply a commercial operation."

"And I have a contract with the owners of that commercial operation. Quatermain growled. "As do you, so I suggest that we cooperate with each other."

"Good luck with that." Lt. Holloway muttered.

"Very well," Newman conceded. "I will see you in the morning." As he strode away he pointed at a couple of tents that had been hastily erected on the lee of a nearby bluff away from the rest of the camp. "Your sleeping quarters, Gentlemen."

Newman was as good as his word; the next day he gave Quatermain and Holloway his full cooperation, stupefyingly so. He walked them through every aspect of the camp in the finest most elaborate detail. Every tent, every hole in the ground, every process step. Everything from cataloging of the finds to the miner's bathroom facilities were toured and annunciated chapter and verse. Quatermain felt as if literally no stone had been left unturned. It was a mentally draining and exhausting experience, and he felt more tired than he did after a day spent hacking his way along a jungle trail. With a muffled groan that might just pass for a "good night" he and Holloway staggered into their respective tents. Quatermain collapsed onto the bedroll and instantly fell into the arms of Morpheus.

Perhaps it was the subtle change in illumination as the light of the partial moon shone through, or the sound of the rough canvas tearing beneath the blade; but Quatermain rolled away just as the large knife arced through the tent and thudded into his now unoccupied bedroll. The hunter cursed himself for allowing himself to be caught sleeping. He hadn't placed any of the usual dry sticks around his tent, or other tricks, that would alert him to the presence of unwanted company. No-one followed the knife through the opening, and he couldn't see any shadow on the tent canopy. Whoever had attacked him had made their throw and assumed the knife had struck home while making good their escape. Quatermain rolled to a crouching stance, grabbed the handle of the knife, gave it a quick twist to release it from the bedroll and stepped out of the tent, scanning the nearby ground for his assailant. A body lay on the ground abut six feet in front of him.

The body groaned.

Quatermain reached the body in a couple of his long strides. Even in the subdued moonlight he could tell from the dark patches that the man's hair was matted with blood. He rolled the man over; his features were obscured by more blood issuing from a knife wound across the face. He had been slashed on a diagonal line from just below his right eye, down across his nose, stopping about an inch from the edge of his mouth. Quatermain didn't need to see the man's disfigured face to recognize the victim. The size and proportions of the body instantly identified him as Adjutant Lt. Holloway. Shouldering the wounded man, Quatermain set of in the direction of one of the tents he'd been painstakingly shown earlier in the day, the camp doctor's tent. Half way between his tent and the medical facility he saw something else lying on the ground that he also recognized, a battered stove-pipe hat.

❋ ❋ ❋

Newman failed to reappear over the next few days. Quatermain spent time split between exploring the camp on his own and sitting alongside the recovering Adjutant. The days soon expanded into a week or more. Quatermain had given little thought to the relative passage of time until on morning when he entered the medical tent to be greeted by a cheery "'Appy Christmas" from the wounded officer whose face was now clear of bandages, although the scar from his wound still seem to pulsate with rage.

"How are you feeling?" Quatermain answered.

The wounded man reached up to his disfigured face, "Well this ain't the best Christmas present I've ever had, but it's one I soon won't forget." The eyes dropped in contemplation, then he looked up again and spoke, Lt. Holloway's voice was low and dark. "Talking of which, where is the bastard?"

"Newman?" Quatermain asked, "So he did this to you?"

"Who else could it bloody well be? Holloway snapped darkly, "Didn't you see 'is 'at lyin' there?"

Quatermain just nodded in confirmation, then he stepped forward and lightly ran his fingers along Holloway's scar.

"What in blazes are you doin'"

"Examining your wound. Interesting angle."

"What's that meant to mean? He's a good foot taller than me. Slashed downward he did. Caught me by surprise."

"The height thing is curious." muttered Quatermain as he looked once again at Holloway who had raised himself from his cot and stood radiating indignation in the center of the medical tent. "Where's the rest of your regiment?"

"Why do you need to know that? Troop movement's is restricted."

"Well for one your Commanding Officer said to give me your full cooperation," with that he pulled the folded sheet of orders from his shirt pocket, "and secondly with all due respect to the medical staff here, I think you should have that," he pointed again at the scar, "looked at by a professional surgeon. We need to find Doctor Young."

Holloway paused for a second, apparently torn between orders and a sense of duty, and maybe something else Quatermain mused. "Laing's Nek," he muttered.

"Pardon?" Quatermain had heard, he was just pushing the man a little to see how he'd respond.

"Laing's Nek. They're headed for a place called Laing's Nek. It's a few 'undred miles from 'ere."

Quatermain tuned and headed out of the tent. As he departed he called back over his shoulder, "Then we better get a move on." Without breaking stride he continued towards his tent, his hand slipped into his jacket pocket and he rolled the small stash of stones residing there in the palm of his hand. "Laing's Nek," he muttered, "the next step, or a diversion?"

JANUARY 1881

As much as Quatermain felt a part of Africa, while he was most at home trasversing its grasslands, navigating its rivers, or hacking his way through seemingly impenetrable jungles; if there was one thing he was guilty of, that was overlooking the sheer size of the continent. He became complacent about the scale of the geography. Even places that were relatively local to each other were in reality separated by significant distances. Such was the case of the route between the mine and Laing's Nek. They may have both been in the Transvaal area of South Africa, but to travel between the two was a good fifteen days walk, and given the roughness of the terrain, not much less on horse back. It only took a couple of days for Quatermain to realize that his mount was less than ideal for the task ahead, the poor creature was past its prime, marginally sway backed, and developing arthritic tendencies. The hunter, aware as much of the animal's discomfort as his own often dismounted and lead the horse on foot, his own well measured pace being not much different than that of the horse. Meanwhile Adjutant Lieutenant John Holloway sat serenely on his young fresh mount that seemed to pick its way over hillocks and shrub with an almost balletic grace.

"Not sure why we bought that nag along," Holloway laughed one afternoon. "You spend more time off it than on. Fact is I 'alf expect you to start carryin' it on your back 'fore long instead of t'other way round."

"The poor animal is not suited to carrying both man and pack. I can make just as good a pace on foot over this terrain as the horse can. I will not let it suffer unnecessarily."

"And I thought you was a jungle man?"

"I'm not sure I take your point, Lieutenant."

"Well you're a famous hunter. A killer of beasts. So why are you concerned with this one so much?"

"Any man who disregards the health of an animal on which he depends is a fool. All creatures deserve respect, the ones who aid us in our daily lives, and especially the ones we hunt."

"Never took you for an emotional man, Quatermain."

"Not emotional, Holloway. Practical." The army man had no response and the two men spent the rest of the day in communable silence. As the sun dropped and the shadows lengthened, the air took on a distinct chill and Quatermain selected a suitable hollow for them to set up camp for the night. Tents were erected and a fire pit dug and ignited to provide warmth against the chill, a heating source for cooking their meal, and a signal to keep predators at bay. Setting up the camp Quatermain noticed that Holloway always seemed to be busy doing something, but never really achieving much. In fact Quatermain had completed setting up the army man's tent after finishing his own. With the camp set, Quatermain called Holloway over to the light of the fire where he examined the bandages over the man's injuries. A look of concern briefly crossed his face as he took in the look and distinctive odor of puss from an infected wound. He carefully unwrapped the dressings and stepped back gagging slightly.

"What is it, man?" asked Holloway.

"How does it feel?" Quatermain asked drawing a line across his own face in imitation of the location of Holloway's scar.

"Hell if know," Holloway grinned. "It don't feel like nothin'."

"And the smell?"

"Don't smell nothin either." Holloway hesitated as if recalling something. "Now you mention it, I can't smell anything. Not the horse, not the grasses. Nothin." A look of panic crossed his scarred face. "What's happening to me Quatermain?"

"The doc who patched you up did a rush job. The wound across your nose has gone septic. It needs to be treated before it spreads across your face and into your eye socket or jaw."

"Think it'll last till we meets up with our boys, and Doc Young can take a look at it.?"

"I'm afraid that may be too late."

"What about goin' back to the mine?"

"We are past the half way point that would take longer than getting to the regiment for treatment. Besides do you wish to place your care back in the hands of the doctor who did such a slip-shod job in the first instance? If he'd followed the guide lines of his profession more carefully you wouldn't be in this condition in the first place."

"Good point." Holloway nodded ruefully, "So what do we do? You saying I'm doomed to let me face rot off?"

Quatermain reached around behind him and pulled a large bladed knife from a sheath on the back of his belt. He raised it in front of the Adjutants' face. Holloway blanched slightly and gulped. "What you planning on doing with that? Gonna put me out of my misery?"

"Just a little jungle surgery." Quatermain flicked the knife away and plunged the blade deep into the flames of the camp fire. "Do you have any alcohol in your bags?"

"It's against regulations." Holloway muttered, never taking his eyes off the blade nestled in the flickering flames.

"I don't think regulations have ever bothered you," Quatermain countered.

"Point taken." Holloway winced at the bad timing of his inappropriate pun. "About the regulations I mean."

"Go get the drink. Sit back down here. Then finish the bottle, or bottles. Drink as much as you can."

"Is it gonna 'urt that much?" Holloway pulled his eyes away from the fire, and stared at Quatermain, his face blanched white.

"More."

Quatermain hadn't lied; Holloway's scream as Quatermain drew the red hot blade of the knife along the depth of the scar that crossed the army man's face was beyond human. The hunter had heard men scream before, scream in fear, scream in pain, or even scream in sheer unbridled terror, but he had never heard a sound like this before; a prolonged discordant symphony of pure agony. He kept his hand steady moving the knife at a measured pace, cutting away infected flesh while simultaneously cauterizing it. The smell of burnt flesh assailed his nostrils, but he too ignored that. The screams continued for what seemed like an eternity after the final cut, even though it was probably less than a minute until Holloway collapsed into a silence built on a foundation of alcohol, pain, and terror. Quatermain dragged the wounded man into his own tent and sat beside him watching him throughout the night.

The night was far from quiet as Quatermain heard the familiar snuffles and snorts of those animals that slithered and scuttled, testing the limits

"I'm afraid that may be too late."

of the camp. The fire did its job. But among the sounds he was certain he'd also caught the occasional note of another familiar step on the rough terrain.

Lieutenant Holloway woke with the first light of day, every movement of his head bought moans of protest, a combination of hangover and lingering pain from Quatermain's impromptu and somewhat drastic medical attentions. Quatermain checked him for a fever, of which there was no sign, and left him to his misery. Stepping out of the tent he carefully examined the ground. What he saw confirmed his suspicions, but the first order of the day was to eat. The hunter rekindled the fire and dug into the packs, retrieving the necessary supplies to cook up some sustenance. They had left the mine supplied with standard army field rations, but along the way Quatermain had made sure to pick specific herbs, plants, and berries to add to the stash. While rations can provide a good base for the man on the move, the application of some field and jungle craft, along with selected flora can turn them into a surprisingly appetizing meal. Carrying two tin plates loaded with his carefully crafted offerings, Quatermain returned to the tent and offered one to Holloway who very slowly and carefully pushed himself up to the sitting position. The effort clearly made him light-headed.

"Smell's good," Holloway remarked. "Can't be compo rations smelling like that. That normally smells like old socks."

"Just the addition of a little local flavoring," Quatermain smiled. "Talking of the locals, looks like we had some visitors last night, there's footprints around the camp fire this morning and they aren't yours or mine."

"Natives?" Holloway looked concerned. "Zulu maybe?"

"Doubt it?' Quatermain mused aloud. "Not unless they were wearing boots."

"Boer?"

"Most likely."

"How they find us?"

"I'm sure your vocal performance under the knife did something to attract their attention."

"So why didn't they dispatch us when they had the chance? Since they declared independence, they've not exactly been kindly towards us British troops."

"Good question. Maybe we'll get our answer tonight."

"Tonight?" Holloway gulped, even though the action resulted in a flash of pain across his facial wound. "You thinking of stickin' around while those buggers are lurkin' out there? You're crazy jungle man."

Quatermain pointed at the wound on the soldiers face. "You still need a day's rest, you can hardly stand up, let alone stay upright on a horse. We head out there we'll be open targets. We stay here; I can control the situation, and maybe get a few answers too."

"I'm not staying around to be the bait in your trap, Quatermain." Holloway pushed him self up. It was the wrong thing to do. What little color had come back to his complexion immediately drained away, his eyes rolled upwards and he fell back to his bedroll unconscious. Quatermain left him to his delirium and to drift in and out of consciousness for the rest of the day while he periodically checked on the Lieutenant amid his preparations for their expected visitors.

At last the day turned to dusk, and dusk turned to dark, and Quatermain waited.

Waited and watched.

The hours passed, and even the hunter began to doubt his instincts.

The muffled curse was low; in fact if Quatermain hadn't been listening for it, he probably wouldn't have heard it. The curse was accompanied by a soft thump as a body hit the ground. Quatermain started to move the instant he heard the exclamation and was out of the tent by the time the body hit the ground. Quatermain was on the man, his knife strategically placed in front of the prone man's face. He got the message and stayed quiet. Together they waited hunter and prey, in the dark until Quatermain was sure that any of the man's companions, if there had been any, had abandoned their mission. As the hint of sunlight started to change the sky, Quatermain pulled the intruder to his feet and prodded him in the back with the point of his knife, driving him in the direction of the tent.

Holloway smiled at the arrival of the duo. "Seem's your little traps worked after all. Must admit I thought the twigs and dry leaves things was a bit obvious."

"It was meant to be," Quatermain responded. "I was counting on whoever was watching the camp seeing me. What they didn't see was the trip snares I set at ankle height. Human nature meant that if they ventured into camp they would be focused on the ground to avoid the twigs and not looking a few inches above it. "

"So what did you catch?"

Quatermain prodded with the knife again, "Want to talk?"

The man shook his head.

"A lone scout by the look of him. No one came to his aid after he tripped. Seems no one is looking for him. Yet. I'd say we have a day or two before anyone considers him missing."

"So what do we do with 'im, then?"

"If he's got no interest in talking to us, he could just leave him hog-tied out here, so he can interact with the local animal predators."

"You wouldn't," the scout stammered.

"It speaks." Holloway remarked with a barely disguised touch of scorn.

Quatermain ignored the soldier's barb and addressed the scout. "Care to explain things to me, or the hyenas, your choice."

"You were correct. I'm a scout. I was sent to track any British troop movements, but all I saw was you two."

"So why did you come into our camp?" Holloway asked.

"Was just trying to listen in, see if you gave anything away while you chatted. But didn't hear anything I didn't already know. Thought I'd sneak in again last night to see if you had any maps, orders, or anything useful I could take back with me. Just to prove that I did my job."

"Well you'll get to see a lot more than that. You're coming with us. What's your name son?"

"What!" Holloway exclaimed, "You're planning on marching him right into camp along side us. He'll see everything."

"Yes he will. But he can also tell your commander anything he wants to know about the Boer positions."

"It'll be too late by then," Holloway groused, "they'll have moved on from where he last was with them."

"True. But it's his choice. Come with us and talk, or take his chances with the hyenas."

"Peiter Van Hausen. And I'll take my chances with you."

The strange little party continued its trek across the plains. Quatermain continued on foot leading his sway backed pony; Van Hausen trudged along behind his bound hands connected to the pony's tail by a ten foot loop of rope. Twenty feet or so further back rode Holloway, who seemingly felt compelled to throw verbal insults at the captive scout on a regular basis. In the evenings they made camp and Quatermain would dress the army man's wounds, but gradually had less and less to do with him, and started to favor the company of the man who politics dictated he should treat as an enemy.

The trio continued in this manner for several more days until they came to within four or so miles of their destination, Laing's Nek. The sight that greeted them there was almost beyond belief.

During his years in Africa, the man known as Allan Quatermain had seen many strange sights, from the magical to the spiritual, from the magnificent to the tardy, from the awe-inspiring to horrors unimaginable, from the inspired to the lunatic; but he couldn't quite figure out how to categorize what greeted his party as the crested a small rise in the grass covered hills.

"What the hell are they doing?" asked an equally stunned Van Hausen.

"Tiffin I imagine," Holloway offered.

"Tiffin?" Van Hausen queried.

"Lunch." Holloway explained.

"Will you just look at them. Such arrogant stupidity." Quatermain shook his head in disgust.

The three men continued to stare at the strange surreal sight in front of them. The slope of the hill that fell away from them petered out into a small flat plateau about fifty feet below where Quatermain, Holloway, and Van Hausen stood. On that patch of grass covered flat land a long table had been set up. It was covered with a fine white linen table cloth and laid with full sets of silverware and what appeared to be fine bone china plates and crystal cut wine glasses. The center of the table was dominated by a large cake stand. Around the table were set a series of folding chairs on which Quatermain estimated sat approximately twenty British officers all of whom were in full dress uniform. Their bright red tunics were crossed by white belts and about half the number were still wearing accompanying bright white pith helmets with gold regimental badges catching the sunlight as the heads moved in animated conversation. They may as well have been signaling the Boer to use them as target practice, and yet they sat as calmly as if they had met for a formal regimental picnic in the grounds of Buckingham Palace. The sound of hooves broke Quatermain's contemplation of the arrogance of Empire. The sound came from just along side him, and he spun just in time to catch sight of Holloway spurring his horse forward. The adjutant grabbed Van Hausen's arm as he sped past and dragged the equally surprised Boer scout along side him, not giving the man a chance to regain his footing or pull himself up onto the horse's back.

Holloway galloped towards the group of officers at the table, and made straight for the man at the head, which Quatermain took to be the senior officer. They were now too far away for the hunter to hear the ensuing exchange, but it was clear from Holloway's actions and gestures that he was proudly delivering one of the enemy into the hands of his superiors and taking full credit for it. Quatermain noticed that the officer in question appeared to ignore Holloway's gesticulations and instead pointed back up the hill in Quatermain's direction. Taking that as a signal Quatermain headed down the hill towards the incongruous table and its occupants. Reaching the officer Quatermain presented his folded orders and introduced himself,

"Allan Quatermain," he nodded slightly in greeting.

"Colonel Dane, Commanding the 3rd Battalion of the 60th Rifles." The officer also nodded as the two men sized each other up warrior to warrior, "How may I be of assistance?"

"You'll find the answer there," Quatermain indicated the folded orders with the Colonel now held in hand. Dane unfolded the well worn paper and read. He let out a slow low whistle which seems out of character for an officer of a presumably aristocratic background. The reaction made Quatermain smile. "You come with some impressive references Mr. Quatermain, but the question remains, how may I be of service?" Before Quatermain could utter a single word in response the officer sat next to Dane crumpled forward as his brains splattered across the pristine white table cloth. Almost before the slain man's head, or what remained of it, hit the table with a resounding thump, Quatermain had grabbed Dane and pulled him under the table. They were quickly joined by Van Hausen who dragged Holloway behind him. From their vantage they saw the legs of two other officers crumble and the red of their uniforms spread across the grasslands. Only then did the other officers react and join them under cover.

"Where the 'ell did that come from?" A stunned Holloway garbled, "I didn't hear no shots."

"We're too far away and the wind's in the wrong direction for the sound to carry here," Quatermain answered. He looked at Van Hausen, "Isn't that right."

"Yes," the captive man answered. "Sniper in the hills."

"You bastard!" Holloway lunged, "You lead us into an ambush."

"Stand down, Lieutenant Holloway," snapped Dane. "That's an order. You lead this man here as your prisoner. He didn't know our position until you brought him here. If there's blame to be had you better look to your self first."

"If there's blame to be had, " Quatermain somberly added, "it's with those uniforms and that ridiculous tea-party. " He nodded in the direction of the table above them.

"But shooting from a distance. Hiding and not declaring hostilities. That's just not how things are done." One of the cowering officers complained.

"Apparently it's how things are done now," Colonel Dane countered with a bitter resignation in his voice.

"This isn't the playing fields of Eton, nor is it Agincourt, nor Waterloo, Gentlemen," Quatermain's voice was calm and carried such authority that all under the table turned towards him. "This is Africa."

❀ ❀ ❀

"So tell me about this Africa of yours," Major General Sir George Pomeroy Colley looked at Quatermain with thinly disguised contempt. "And why an Englishman like you would get involved with these," he paused, clearly struggling for a suitable term, "rebels?"

Before answering, Quatermain thought back to the conversation he'd had with Colonel Dane on the way over to the Major General's tent. A lot had happened in this part of Africa while Quatermain had been away. Following the Boer declaration of independence for the Transvaal in December 1880 the British had suffered a series of disastrous defeats in attempting to regain the territory. On the 20 December 1880, Lieutenant-Colonel Philip Robert Anstruther and elements of his regiment, the 94th, had marched from Lydenburg to Pretoria, but the force was stopped by Boers who courteously required the "Red Soldiers" to turn back. Anstruther equally courteously refused at which the column was devastated by rifle fire from the surrounding Boer ambush. Of the 259 in the column, 155 officers and men became casualties as did some of the women accompanying the regiment.

Instead of waiting for the reinforcements, the British High Commissioner for South East Africa, Major General Sir George Pomeroy Colley, the man now waiting for Quatermain's response, had assembled what troops he could and rushed forward, claiming to be moving to relieve the British garrisons in the Transvaal. Colley had dispatched an ultimatum to the Boers and, on its rejection, advanced towards the Transvaal border. They were now in the initial British camp located some four miles short of Laing's Nek, a ridge in the foothills of the Drakensberg

Mountains. Dane explained that at an elevation of 5400 to 6,000 ft. it was the lowest part of a ridge which slopes from Majuba to the Buffalo River, and was the main artery of communication between Durban and Pretoria. The British Natal Field Force, commanded by General Colley, currently numbered around 1,216 officers and men, including five companies of the 58th Regiment, five companies of the 3rd Battalion, the 60th Rifles, about 150 cavalry of the Mounted Squadron, a party of Royal Navy sailors and 4 guns of the Royal Artillery. According to what intelligence the British had managed to gather opposing them was a force of Boer fighters, under the command of Commandant-General Joubert that had about 2,000 men in the area, with at least 400 fortifying the heights directly around Laing's Nek.

Before responding, Quatermain glanced around the tent taking in his surroundings. Despite the Major General's patronizing tone, it was clear that this was no ordinary soldier, but a man with an open mind and an appreciation of the natural world. Several watercolors, mainly of the English moors and the French coast were propped up against trunks bringing a splash of color to the military decor. An easel nearby and a stack of sketchbooks showed that Colley himself was the artist. The books scattered around the tent covered a variety of subjects from chemistry to politics, while the novel on the nightstand by the officer's cot appeared to be a Russian text. Quatermain cleared his throat. "This isn't my Africa, but nor is it yours, nor is it Queen Victoria's." This statement bought a few shocked gasps and exclamations of "I say!" from amongst the staff officers collected in the tent. "But nor is it the Boers," Quatermain continued. "I'm as loyal a subject to the crown as you'll find on this continent, but Africa is too large, and too primal for anyone to claim. It houses the fantastic and the unimaginable; it is the cauldron of mankind and brings out the best and the worst of us. This squabble over territory and mining rights is insignificant but if you insist on pursuing it do not treat Africa lightly and do not underestimate those who call it home. Your rules don't apply here, follow them at your peril."

Major-General Colley smiled behind his impressive whiskers. "I too know Africa, Elephant Hunter, for I have served most of my career on this continent. I know of you too, your exploits, and you thirst for adventure. This isn't an adventure, Mr. Quatermain, it's a military campaign, and it will be conducted as such. The orders you furnished me asked for me to provide assistance in you conducting your investigation. You have highly placed and influential friends. I will be happy to provide that assistance after we have secured the passage through Laing's Nek. In the mean time

I suggest that you attach yourself to Colonel Dane's command and make your self useful tomorrow.

The morning of January 28th dawned like many others for Allan Quatermain, sleeping under the stars of the African sky. He'd passed up the offer of a tent, preferring his own company and the expanse of the fields. The hunter had snapped awake, stretched, and raised himself to his feet, sweeping his gaze over his surroundings. The rows of conical military tents, once again made of a bleached white canvas, stood in organized regimented rows across the field. Outside each tent stood a tripod of Martini Henry single shot breech loading rifles with their long sword bayonets lashed together. No-one else was yet awake. Quatermain silently walked through the camp and passed the few men on watch without them noticing his passage. He ventured out in search of his own breakfast, preferring the small game over the army rations. He'd been gone a few hours when the noise reached him. The dull thump and bass reverberation of an artillery piece being fired.

Major-General Colley had declared war on the Boers at Laing's Nek

As he crested the hill at the rear of the camp, Quatermain's senses were assaulted by the cacophony of a full artillery barrage. The single initial shot had been joined by four nine-pound guns and the two seven-pound guns as they laid siege to the Boer positions at the summit of the hill across the other side of the field which had been witness to the singular tea-party the day before. Lined up behind the cannon resplendent in their red jackets, blue trousers with red piping, and white pith helmets and belts, stood the ranks of five companies of the 58th Regiment along side five companies of the 3rd Battalion, the 60th Rifles, waiting for the command to commit themselves to the fight. Quatermain scanned the line searching for Colonel Dane, and soon found him. Stood next to Dane was a familiar rotund figure somewhat lacking in height when compared to the other soldiers, Lieutenant Holloway.

"Good Morning, Colonel," Quatermain shouted over the noise of the cannon as he strode up to stand between the two men. "Looks like it's going to be an interesting morning."

"Morning, Quatermain," Colonel Dane returned the greeting also raising his voice. "This is not your fight, sir. You do not need to accompany us into the field."

Quatermain nodded in the direction of Holloway, "For the moment, I go where he goes." He turned to Holloway. "When this day is over I need you to introduce me to that surgeon of yours. Let us hope that he doesn't have too many calling on his services."

Holloway ignored the remark.

"Where's Van Hausen?" Quatermain asked.

"That spy's tied up in one of the tents," Holloway snorted. "We'll deal with 'im later."

The noise stopped as abruptly as it started. The sudden silence was as unnatural as the noise. It was as if Africa suddenly took a breath. A pause before the madness. Then a whistle blew and the ranks of the red jackets advanced.

What had been rolling fields of Transvaal grassland was now, thanks to the bombardment, a mass of torn and broken ground. The carefully regimented ranks soon broke as men stumbled and fell. Without a shot being fired by the Boers, the British commanders had managed to cripple their own advance. Curses and shouted commands were intermixed with shouts of pain as men twisted ankles in the pock marked surface. Grass had been replaced by mud further slowing process. Quatermain shouted across to Colonel Dane, "In what way did this make sense?"

"By the book," Dane replied, "standard tactical procedure to soften up the enemy."

"What enemy?" Quatermain waved his arm in the direction of the stumbling army before him; there wasn't a Boer to be seen.

Fifteen minutes of stumbling bought the ranks of the 58th and 60th to the foot of the hill that sloped up to where it was believed that the enemy waited. Here they rested while order was restored.

"Now you'll see some action," Dane called, his voice tinged with excited anticipation.

"Geez, he's a cheerful bugger when he's facing death," muttered Holloway.

The sound of bugles reached Quatermain from further down the line and he turned to watch a squadron of mounted cavalry ride into sight and gallop up the slope of the nearby hill, clearly hoping to outflank the Boers at the top of the hill in front of where Dane had stationed his troops. It seemed that Major General Colley had a plan after all. The riders thundered up the hill, again without meeting any opposition. Quatermain could almost picture what happened next. Emboldened by the lack of opposition the horses crested the summit of the nearby hill and disappeared from sight. It was then that the rifle fire started. As they rode over the summit the men and horses had been perfectly silhouetted against the early morning sky, and as they rode down the reverse side of the slope they were an easy target for the entrenched Boer fighters on the reverse of the slope. Quatermain and his companions watched as wounded men and horses straggled back over the summit in an unordered withdrawal that smacked of panic. Colonel Dane wasn't about to let the sight of the failed flanking maneuver undermine the confidence of his troops and immediately ordered them forward to attack before they had time to think about what they had seen.

They advanced with bugles playing, drums beating, and regimental flags flying in the breeze.

That's when the shooting really started.

Quatermain cursed himself for getting caught up in this stupidity, and vowed to himself that he had two objectives that day, to get out alive, and if possible make sure that Holloway got out alive too. Not because he liked the man or had any obligation to him, quite the opposite in fact, but he needed Holloway to lead him to the diamond smugglers, and he had an obligation to DeBeers, and more importantly one to his son, and Harry was more important to him than any colonial entanglement. He would not die today. It was as simple as that.

But other men died. The fire from the Boers at the top of the hill was precise. They took their time and selected their targets with care. These were men who habitually carried rifles to guard their animal stocks, and had a life time's experience of marksmanship to call on. The first to fall were the men carrying the regimental colors. Designed to be a rallying point in the tumult and confusion of battle, they had on this day become a brightly colored target. Yet as one man fell, another rushed to take his place and raise the flag again. Sheer force of numbers kept the line moving upwards until at last the British troops reached the summit of the hill above them. As Quatermain had surmised from the fate of the earlier cavalry charge on the adjacent hill, the Boers were entrenched on the reverse side of the slope, patiently waiting. The enemy was almost impossible to see, no brightly colored uniforms or flags for them, instead the typical Boer fighter wore what they wished, generally a tan jacket, trousers and slouch hat with a bandolier carrying ammunition for their ever-present hunting rifle. Those same rifles that continued to rain death. Reaching the summit Quatermain had dropped to a crouch to reduce his silhouette and as he did so he reached out and grabbed the belts of the two men either side of him, Holloway on his right, and Colonel Dane on his left. He dropped, pulling the two soldiers down with him and rolled over the summit and down the reverse slope until they stopped behind a small rise topped with tall grasses that provided some cover.

"Stay down," Quatermain hissed above the whine of bullets that flew over their heads.

"…another man…raised the flag…"

"We need figure out where those trenches are and the strength of the opposition," Dane responded. "Holloway you go right and I'll go left."

"I ain't goin' nowhere," Holloway responded. "You 'eard Mr. Quatermain. I'm staying right 'ere."

"Goddamit, man. That's an order."

"Ah don't care. Court martial me if you like. You know it won't stick. I'm not 'ere to fight your bloomin' war."

"I'll go," Quatermain cursed himself for saying it.

"This isn't your fight, Quatermain,"Dane looked at the hunter, "and I can't order you."

Right on both counts, Quatermain thought to himself, but he liked the Colonel and felt obliged to him. As for Holloway, he wished he could just push him out into the field of fire, but he'd made that vow to himself. Quatermain knew he was protecting the wrong man, and there was nothing he could do about it. He looked at the Colonel and just nodded.

"OK, on the count of three. One... Two... Goddamit! No..." Dane raced out from behind the cover and into the line of fire. Quatermain looked to see what had caused the Colonel to act impulsively. The regimental colors had once again fallen, perhaps for the forth of fifth time, Quatermain had lost count; but this time no-one stepped forward to pick them up, for all around the downed flag were only the bodies of dead men. Dane was heading for the flag. Quatermain ran after him.

"Colonel, leave it!" Quatermain didn't hear the shot, but he saw the effects as Colonel Dane of the 3rd Battalion 60th Rifles staggered back three steps. The wounded man pulled himself upright and pushed forward only to stagger again as another shot hit him in chest. The Colonel pulled himself along the ground, crawling over the bodies until his hand grasped the pole of the downed flag.

Quatermain cursed as he ran, "Damned fool." He wasn't sure if he was referring to the Colonel or himself. How he managed to reach the wounded officer without incurring the same fate was a mystery, but even Quatermain's luck had to run out at some point. As he grabbed Dane's belt and started to lift the wounded officer, his leg gave way from under him. Falling, Quatermain cursed his age. As he slid to the floor he noticed the blood starting to seep into his trouser leg, "Damn." Then came the pain, and the blackness.

"Come on my friend, stay with me."

Allan Quatermain opened his eyes to see the dull brown outfit of a Boer soldier standing over him. Van Hausen.

The Boer slipped his arm around Quatermain's chest and pulled him to his feet. Quatermain cried out in pain as he put his weight on the wounded leg and almost collapsed again. He leaned against his former walking companion. "It went straight through the muscle. I bandaged it but you need to get it looked at." Van Hausen said.

"Colonel Dane?" Quatermain tried to turn back to where the officer lay.

"He's gone. I'm sorry. He was a good officer. Treated me well. Unlike Holloway."

"Holloway." Quatermain pointed in the direction of the clump of grass that had provided them temporary cover before the Colonel's mad dash. "Need to get to Holloway."

"OK," Van Hausen said. "I've no idea what the connection is between you two, but I'll get you there. The fighting has moved on so we should be safe. Most of the red jackets are on the run back to their camp. But that won't help them much, as the group that freed me are keeping things busy there as well." The Boer scout and the hunter moved slowly across the slope ignored by both the living and the dead as they headed in search of the coward with the hidden agenda. Holloway was exactly where Quatermain had left him.

Holloway stared up in disbelief as Van Hausen appeared before him supporting the wounded Quatermain. "You bastard," Holloway snapped, but made no move to confront his enemy.

"You're not worth the trouble to deal with," Van Hausen spat at Holloway, "but this man…" he gently placed Quatermain down next to Holloway, "… this man deserves respect. See to it that he gets medical attention. If he doesn't I will find out, and I will come for you." Van Hausen reached his hand down and placed it on Quatermain's shoulder, "Farewell hunter, I hope that we meet again under better circumstances. I would like to call you friend one day."

The Boer disappeared from view, and Quatermain felt the darkness returning. As he slipped once again into unconsciousness he heard the faint sounds of the Cease Fire being sounded from the British camp on the other side of the hill. After three hours, the battle for Laing's Nek was over.

Blood, shit, chloroform, and more combined to form the foul miasma that provided the stimulus to reignite Allan Quatermain's senses. The smell was quickly followed by pain. Pain from his wounded leg. Quatermain grimaced but kept his eyes shut. Only a low moan escaped his lips, but none seemed to notice as the hum of conversation continued around him. He guessed he must be in one of the hospital tents.

"Can't you do some'at about him while he's out of it, Doc?" Quatermain recognized Holloway's voice from the foot of his bed.

"Maybe we could use him?" A more cultured, educated voice responded. Maybe this was the elusive Doctor Young.

"What?" Holloway sounded confused. "As a courier? No point, he won't be going back to Blighty anytime soon. He lives 'ere in Africa. Loves the place he does. Something of a legend around the Dark Continent from what I 'eard."

"Not as a courier, you imbecile," the Doctor sounded exasperated. "But as a distraction. We're going to be shipping a lot of wounded back home and I don't need him or anyone else snooping around. But, as you say, he's something of a celebrity in these parts. He can help us draw attention away from our little scheme."

"Not bad, Doc," Holloway's voice now reflecting a degree of admiration, "so what's your plan?"

Quatermain's eye's snapped open and he moaned a little louder.

"Ah you're awake, Mr. Quatermain. Good."

Quatermain looked up at the figure leaning over him. The Doctor was tall and thin, almost cadaverous in looks. His eyes sunken into a thin face with a hawk like nose. The face looked racked with fatigue, with dark rims around the eyes. The body sagged a little, and he constantly shifted his stance as a result of having been on his feet for an extended period. The Doctor's clothes were covered in stains from a variety of bodily fluids. He looked like the Grim Reaper and as Quatermain stared back at those sunken eyes he saw nothing to change that impression.

Most Doctors he knew were like his son, creatures of compassion and empathy as well as healing. This man wasn't any of those things. The eyes were as cold as the void with no spark of humanity in them. This man wasn't a healer, he was a surgeon who operated not to save lives but to make use of them for his own ends.

Quatermain had fixed on the word 'courier' he'd overheard. So that was how it worked. The army surgeon would use a wounded soldier, either slice into him, or better yet sew up a battlefield wound with a package of uncut diamonds inside. Pack the man back to England. Then on his own return from duty call the soldier for a check-up reopen the wound and remove the contraband. Simple, efficient, and cruel. But did the wounded warriors know what they were being used for? And where did the diamonds come from? Holloway. It had to be. All Quatermain had to do now was prove it without getting himself used as a 'distraction.' Quatermain raised himself up on his elbows and nodded towards the foot of the bed indicating his wounded leg. "So what's the news Doctor…" He left the sentence hanging hoping for the surgeon to provide his name. He wasn't disappointed.

"Young. It's Doctor Young."

"Ah. Lieutenant Holloway spoke highly of you, during our journey here from the diamond mines." No reaction.

"The leg wound was a through and through shot. It was stitched up on the afternoon after the battle, but I am afraid that it may go bad. I may have to open it up again just to be sure it's been properly attended to."

"So you didn't do the initial treatment?" Quatermain asked.

"No. Immediate post-engagement procedures are performed in-situ by the field-surgeons. I oversee the hospital and check for any necessary surgery required."

Convenient, thought Quatermain. This gave Young the opportunity to only pick the best candidates for couriers and he could transfer the diamonds under controlled circumstances. "When will you know if you need to administer to my wounds?"

"I have plans to attend to you tomorrow. Mr. Quatermain." The Doctor turned on his unsteady feet and headed to the next bed.

"See you around, Quatermain., Holloway sneered and followed his companion in crime leaving Quatermain to plan.

The Hunter sensed the movement beside him. Someone was stood at the right side of his bed. He slowly let his left arm drop over the side as if shifting in his sleep. The hand searched the floor for anything that might be used as a weapon. All he found was a blood stained rag. He picked it up anyway. Shifting again into fiend slumber he waited for the moment to strike. The presence at his side leaned over the medical cot closing the gap to his intended victim. Quatermain's eyes snapped open and his left arm flew upwards dropping the rag on the bed as it went, The hunter's grip was strong and his left hand clasped itself around the throat of his attacker. In a synchronized movement Quatermain's right arm swept across the bed grabbing the rag, which he immediately stuffed into the figure's mouth chocking off any possible sound. Once his quarry was immobilized and silenced Quatermain took a good look at who he'd caught. Tall, thin, and cadaverous in appearance.

"Doctor Young. Come to finish off your treatment no doubt."

The figure squirmed as if trying to pull away and shook his head. Through the bloody improvised gag he tried to speak. The words were unclear but it carried the resonance of an impassioned denial. Enough to make Quatermain take another look at the man. There was no white coat. The body posture was straighter than Young's and the early morning light filtering into the hospital tent revealed a pale almost parchment like skin tone. And the eyes. There was a something in those eyes, a hint of recognition and pleading. Quatermain dropped his chock hold and pulled the rag from the man's mouth.

"My God. Charles Newman."

The tall man nodded as he rubbed his throat and worked his tongue to get moisture back into his mouth. "At your service, Mr. Quatermain." He bowed slightly.

"We thought you dead."

"I was left for dead, but it seems that the Good Lord had other plans for me."

"Did you attack Holloway?"

"That I cannot deny. I most certainly did. The night after your inspection of the mine I resolved to tell you of my suspicions. I apologize for being so terse and uncommunicative during your visit, but Holloway was ever present during your tour and I needed an opportunity to talk to you alone. I may not be the most sociable or impressive man, but, I am, above all other things, a loyal employee of DeBeers, and you were operating on a mandate from my superiors in London. I was honor bound to share my concerns with you."

"So why attack Holloway?"

"As I approached your tent that evening, I came across the Lieutenant also heading in the direction of your tent, with a large knife in his hand. He was so focused on his task that I don't believe he heard me behind him. Surmising that his intent was to do you some harm, I picked up a large piece of timber that was on the ground nearby, and swung it at his head. Not being a physical man used to violence I can only guess that I did not have the requisite strength to deliver an effective blow as it hardly seem to have any effect, other than to alert him to my presence. He quickly spun around and slashed me across the arm with that knife of his making me drop the timber."

Newman pulled up the sleeve of his tattered jacket to reveal a livid ragged scar across his forearm. Before Quatermain could ask any questions he continued his narrative. "As I staggered back Holloway sheathed his knife, picked up the timber, and swung it back at me. I guess you could say I was hoisted by my own petard as he connected with the side of my head, knocking my hat off, and sending me into oblivion. For I recall nothing until waking up in the gully of a dried up ditch a few days later covered in a mass of stones, branches, and dried fauna, where I had apparently been left for dead."

"You said that Hollway sheathed the knife. So how did you cut his face?"

"I didn't inflict any wounds on the Lieutenant. As I said I'm not a fighting man."

"Damn it. I'm an idiot," Quatermain reprimanded himself. "I knew there was something off about the angle of that wound. He slashed himself across the face to make it look like you attacked him."

"But I did attack him. So why would he feel the need to do that?"

"In case you were found, then he could cite self-defense."

"That seems an awfully drastic thing to do."

"Drastic and foolish, he nearly succumbed to an infection from it. Maybe I should have let it take him."

"I will say," said Newman,."It must take a certain amount of courage to draw a knife across your own face."

"There's nothing courageous about self-mutilation," snorted Quatermain, "especially in the service of deception. The man has repeatedly shown himself to be a self serving coward, and a criminal." Quatermain looked at Newman suspiciously. "Did you know about the diamond smuggling?"

"I had my suspicions that he and my cousin were partnered in some nefarious scheme. I hadn't figured out exactly what it was until your arrival. Your mission and the message from the DeBeers management provided the context that clarified things for me. Given the large volume of unprocessed diamonds we uncover every day the amount that they could smuggle is an insignificant percentage overall, but it would still be enough to make a man very wealthy."

"Doctor Young is your cousin. I should have noted the family resemblance before."

"Exactly."

"So where are the Doctor and the Lieutenant this morning? I must admit I was expecting an unpleasant visit from them at some stage during the night."

"That's why, once I heard you were also in the camp, that I came to find you Mr. Quatermain. It seems that neither my relative or his companion in crime are to be found."

🌿 🌿 🌿

"They are headed where?" Major General Sir George Pomeroy Colley was incredulous.

"Towards Zulu territory, sir," replied a nervous young Adjutant.

"Damn them!" The Major General's anger reverberated around his tented headquarters. He looked at Quatermain. "And you're sure you can catch them? We have enough trouble with these rebels, the last thing we need is some stupid incident that will spark another Zulu uprising."

"Yes, sir," Quatermain responded. "But I estimate they have a six hour lead, and the longer we stand around debating what action to take they harder it will be to catch up with them before they stumble into somewhere they shouldn't be."

"So how many soldiers will you need, Quatermain?"

"None will be necessary, Sir. Thank you for the offer. I'll be fine."

"As you wish. Despite that scoundrel Hollway's involvement I view this as a matter for DeBeers and its agents rather than the military." The Major General looked straight at the Adjutant. "Make sure that the gentleman is as fully provisioned as he needs."

The Adjutant snapped of a smart brisk salute along with a crisp "Yes Sir." He then turned to Quatermain and Newman. "Follow me, Gentlemen."

The party left the command tent and briefly stopped. "Don't worry Newman, I'll catch up with them," Quatermain reassured the Mine Agent.

"Oh I'm coming with you."

"But you said you weren't a physical man. Far from a man of action if I recall."

"But I have an obligation to my employers to see this through. I'm sure you understand that."

Quatermain nodded, "I certainly do." With that he headed to the edge of the camp, as the Adjutant scurried off to collect various supplies. The officer caught up with Quatermain and Newman about thirty minutes later on the far side of the camp. Quatermain was crouched down examining the ground around him. When the Adjutant spoke, Quatermain ignored him as he focused on his task.

"I'll take those," Charles Newman offered, reaching out his hand to relieve the man of the two packs he was carrying.

"They are both heavy packs, sir." The soldier reported. "One for each of you."

"I'll take both," Newman insisted. "I may look like I can't hold much, but despite my frame I have a certain amount of strength; plus it would be more beneficial to leave Mr. Quatermain unencumbered so he may employ his tracking skills more freely." The Adjutant just shrugged and handed over the two packs without further comment.

"They definitely left camp at this spot," Quatermain looked up at Newman. "Are you ready?"

"Lead on, Mr. Quatermain."

The earlier supposition that the two fugitives were headed in the direction of Zulu territory seemed to be confirmed by their tracks. Since the British Invasion of Zululand three years earlier and the defeat of the Zulu leadership the once proud nation had splintered into many small kingdoms and each remained disputed territory. The Anglo-Zulu War may have technically been over, but tensions remained and the presence of two English fugitives would only exacerbate the situation.

They found the first body about four hours after leaving camp. It was lying in a gully at the edge of a wooded copse. Quatermain had pointed at the shape in the grass without a word. Newman gasped, "Is it...?"

"Neither of them I'm afraid," Quatermain responded as he approached the edge of the gully and looked down to get a clearer view of the deceased.

Newman soon joined him, "A Zulu warrior. That will cause problems."

Quatermain shook his head, "Not a warrior yet."

Newman looked again, "My God he's just a boy."

"I'd surmise he was undergoing some coming of age or training ritual. He has his spear and shield, but not the adornments of a full fighting man."

"So why?" Newman shook his head sadly.

"Two desperate men encountering a culture that they don't understand and despise. They saw a threat where there was none."

Newman slid down the gully to examine the young man's body. He gently rolled the corpse over and pointed to a large gash across the chest. "Knife wound."

"Exactly right," the voice came from behind Quatermain. "Don't move, stay exactly where you are Quatermain. And you cousin."

"Doctor Young," Quatermain replied. "I thought you would be long gone by now."

"So did I, hunter, but things don't always go the way that you plan them."

"Where's your knife-wielding companion?"

"He's nearby."

Quatermain started to slowly turn his head in an attempt to glance behind him at the Doctor. He heard the click of a revolver hammer being drawn back, and decided to stay still. At least for a few seconds. As he had turned his head Quatermain had sensed something at the periphery of his vision. He didn't know exactly what he'd seen. But he knew it represented an opportunity. Quatermain dropped his head further down until his chin touched his chest, apparently in an involuntary gesture of further defeat. Then he rolled forward dropping over the edge into the gully. As he rolled he struck out backwards with his feet and smashed them into Young's shins. The Doctor let out a scream of pain and dropped the gun. Quatermain hit the bottom of the gully and stood up, pivoted and raced back up the slope towards the cursing, limping, Doctor. He used the momentum of his run up the slope to carry him over the top of the slope and drive himself headlong into his opponent. They fell together. Both scrabbling for the gun that lay tantalizingly just out of reach. As they rolled Young proved to be as slippery as a snake twisting and turning his thin body making it almost impossible for Quatermain to keep a hold. With one frantic twist Young broke free, rolled away and stood up. As Quatermain rose to his feet to challenge him, Young stomped hard down on Quatermain's leg. Right on top of the recent wound. The pain raced through Quatermain's body from the damaged leg and the wound opened and started to bleed again. He dropped to one knee. Young cackled in delight, bent over and picked up the fallen firearm. With methodical intent he pointed it at the half kneeling Quatermain.

"No tricks, this ti—"

The point of a Zulu spear protruded from his chest. Young looked down puzzled. As his life ebbed away from him he turned to see his cousin, Charles Newman, stood on the edge of the gully the shield of a young Zulu in one hand, while his other hand was empty.

Newman passed his expiring relative without a word or second glance. He stooped, put his arm around Quatermain and pulled him up, supporting him as they took to the shade of the trees. Once under cover Newman lowered Quatermain, and took his own knife and cut away the blood matted trouser leg that was clinging to Quatermain's wound. "It looks bad, Quatermain, it will need sewing up again."

"At least no one will try and stick diamonds in it."

Newman ignored the feeble attempt at humor, "I need to get help."

"Help is here," Quatermain nodded and pointed indicating that Newman should look behind him. A line of six large Zulu warriors stood staring at them.

"Oh my." Newman was flustered, "Listen, we didn't... You know, the boy... It wasn't..."

"The one who took my son has received his punishment," the largest warrior responded in perfect English.

"Holloway," Quatermain said.

"If that was the short soldier's name. He may have worn your Queen's uniform, but he was no warrior. He was the killer of children, and he met his fate like the coward he was."

"What did you..." Newman started to ask.

"Leave it," Quatermain said. "Let Africa be Africa, and don't ask too many questions."

"Wise words," the tall warrior responded. "Your injury looks bad. We will bind it and get you to your people."

"My people," Quatermain laughed. "I don't have people, I have this." We waved his arm around him. "I have Africa."

"I heard the tall thin one call you 'Quatermain'," the warrior continued. "You are the one that some call the Pale Hunter."

Quatermain nodded. "I am sorry for the loss of your son. It is a pain that that no father should have to bear." And with those words he slipped once more into the depths of unconsciousness.

❋ ❋ ❋

Charles Newman dropped the bag of uncut diamonds on the carved mahogany desk of his superior in the London office of DeBeers, where it landed with a satisfying thud. He used his one good arm to indicate the bag, the other being in a sling, the result of getting the ragged scar on his forearm the correct medical attention it deserved. "Herein lies the sum total of all the stones recovered from various wounded men of the 60th Rifles. They deserved better than to be used as common mules by unscrupulous men such as Young and Holloway."

"Quite so." The gruff voice responded. "And what of the man who bought the scoundrels to justice. We haven't heard anything of him since his original departure from these offices."

"His message was that his obligation was fulfilled, and now it was your turn to do the same," Newman reported.

"He couldn't deliver such a message himself?" The man behind the desk asked.

"He prefers the Dark Continent to the dark soot laden streets of the capital, Sir," Newman responded, "but he did have a suggestion. The company clearly needs a more highly skilled practitioner in the position of company surgeon at the mines." Newman raised his damaged arm. "And from personal experience I would second that recommendation. The Hunter suggested that you would know of a young man who may be suitable for that role once his studies are complete."

THE END

WRITING "STONES OF BLOOD."

The idea for this story started over a plate of egg, bacon, beans, and black pudding. In fact it started in the very Covent Garden restaurant where I have Allan Quatermain meet his son at the story's outset. We were at the end of a family trip to the UK and had one day to do as much of London as possible before our return flight. What better way to start a day like that than with a full English breakfast? We ended up in Henry's Restaurant overlooking the cobbled streets of Covent Garden and all I could think about was how would Allan Quatermain react to being back on these London streets? What would pull him back out of Africa to the capital of the British Empire? His son.

Looking at the chronology of when Haggard's Quatermain stories are set there is a gap from the end of King Solomon's Mines (1880) to The Ancient Allan (1882) where I felt he could make such a return trip. Quatermain's son, Harry's death from smallpox while working in a hospital is dated around 1884, so having him at the early stages of his medical career also seemed to fit.

Of course you can't think about London in the 1880s without thinking about Sherlock Holmes (well I can't anyway). The Hansoms of John Clayton, our local Sherlock Holmes society, of which both my wife and I are members, keeps a chronological list of Holme's cases, and according to that Holmes' first recorded case, "The Gloria Scott," took place in 1880. Other sources suggest that Holmes took up residence in Baker Street early the following year, so it seemed logical to me that he might be out and about checking out potential lodgings in late 1880. And if Quatermain and the young Holmes were in town at the same time, I just had to have them meet.

But what would bring them together? Much of the British attention at the time was focused on events in South Africa, mainly the recent Zulu uprisings and the threatened revolt in the Transvaal of the Boer farmers wanting independence. Underscoring all this was the discovery of rich diamond deposits in the area and the following "diamond rush" that had started in 1869. —I had my story.

I did deviate from history on one specific point. In 1880 the DeBeers Company wasn't yet in existence. The company we know as DeBeers was formed in 1888 through the amalgamation of the two leading mining companies of the time. The name DeBeers comes from the surname of the

Boer farmers on whose land the initial diamond finds were made in 1869. I decided to use the name anyway as it's so well known and it conjures up immediate connections to South African diamond mining.

Returning Quatermain to Africa for the majority of the story it seemed inevitable that, given the timing, he would get caught up in the events of the short-lived First Boer War that was fought between December 1880 and March 1881. What is generally referred to as The Boer War usually only references the second, somewhat longer, conflict (1899-1902).

The Battle of Laing's Nek was one of the decisive engagements of the First Boer War and happened pretty much as I described it. The officers did sit down for "tiffin' in full dress uniform in an open field. If you do an internet search of the Laing's Nek battle it is one of the first images that pops up in the results. It was so crazy I just had to include it. While I changed some of the details to get my characters, and their units, into the places I wanted them to be during the battle, the overall strategy and ebb and flow of the battle is accurate. Laing's Nek was a major defeat for the British and changed the way they went into war after that. This was the last time a British regiment would take its colors into battle. The 60th Rifles that I use throughout the story were at Laing's Nek and are still in action under the name The Royal Green Jackets.

Major General Sir George Pomeroy Colley KCSI CB CMG was the commanding officer that day, and other than having one of the best Victorian names, was a fascinating character. He was a renaissance man, politician, diplomat, soldier, artist, and scholar. He was killed in February 1881 during one of the final skirmishes of the First Boer War, and I wish I'd discovered him earlier.

I guess that's one of the frustrations of writing historical fiction. History is full of fascinating characters that surpass anything you can make up, yet you don't always get to give them the stage they deserve within the confines of a particular story or time frame. Meanwhile great fictional characters are nearly always adaptable and open up a world of possibilities, and that what's makes working with Allan Quatrain so much fun, he'll always have Africa, and we'll be along for adventure.

ALAN J. PORTER —Writer, and award-winning editor, Alan J. Porter, has written adventures featuring Sherlock Holmes, Allan Quatermain, Houdini, and private eye Rick Ruby; as well as his own New Pulp adventurers, The Raven and The Lotus Ronin.

His pop-culture non-fiction work has featured properties such as Batman, Star Trek, The Beatles, and James Bond. He has also written comics for Tokyopop, BOOM Studios, Marvel, Disney, and Kid Domino.

A CLASSIC HERO REBORN

British adventure writer, H. Rider Haggard's most popular fictional character was Alan Quatermain, the irascible African big game hunter. As the hero of the classic KING SOLOMON'S MINES, Quatermain immediately fired the imagination of readers across the world and created an instant demand for more of his adventures.

Now Airship 27 Productions answers that on-going demand by presenting two brand new Alan Quatermain novellas each filled with plenty of suspense, action and exotic African locales. When a French riverboat pilot discovers elephant ivory suffused with gold, it sends the expert guide on a quest to find a fabled elephant's graveyard to learn the answer to the "GOLDEN IVORY" by Alan J. Porter.

Next a naïve American lad follows Quatermain deep into the jungle to find eight missing white women only to uncover an ancient evil capable of possessing the bodies of its victim's in Aaron Smith's chilling "TEMPLE OF LOST SOULS."

Here are complete tal...
fans an...
to one of the ...

www.ingramcontent.com/pod-product-compliance
Lightning Source LLC
Chambersburg PA
CBHW051129260626
47170CB00005B/1739